"Hard-hitting and well-knit—the find of the month."
— *Time*

"Fast and exciting."
— *The New Yorker*

"Even Dodge's excellent earlier books have hardly prepared one for the pure virtuosity of narrative excitement which he reveals here."
— *The New York Times*

"Dazzling scenery and some equally dazzling doings en route."
— *San Francisco Chronicle*

"Fine, hard-packed, hard-hitting prose."
— *Anthony Boucher*

"Plentiful action, information, colorful backgrounds… Exciting."
— *The Saturday Review of Literature*

"Very adept weaving of uncommon stuffs and all in all your only probable complaint will be that at the end there isn't any more. First rate."
— *New York Herald Tribune Book Review*

"Accelerated and absorbing."
— *Kirkus Reviews*

A dim light glowed over the stairway that led to the second floor. It was a shaky thing, added on after the building had been turned into a pension, and it swung under me with each step. I went up heavily and slowly. At the top, there was a short hall with four doors. One, which was open, led to a bathroom. Two of the others, badly fitted in their frames, showed no cracks of light. The third did. I pushed at it.

It swung open. I followed it in, barely catching myself from falling. Jeff, sitting at a table on which all my stuff was spread out, looked up at me, grinning his wolf grin. The belly-gun lay near his hand.

"Well, well," he said. "Junior again. Back for a rematch?"

I blinked at him. He had the cuttings spread out in front of him, and was trying to line them up into some kind of sequence. He looked so pleased with himself that I guessed he hadn't got far enough along to find out that what he had didn't mean anything.

I weaved over to the table and reached clumsily for the slips with my left hand. He didn't bother with the gun. I looked too easy for that. When he stood up to smack me, I hooked a right at his chin, as hard as I could throw it. He went headfirst over the back of his chair and hit the wall. Before he could get up, I landed on his chest and was softening him up with both hands, taking out on him not only the sore throat and legs he had left me but all I had put up with from Naharro. It didn't do Jeff any good, but it helped me.

After he stopped struggling, I climbed off and recovered the things he had taken out of my pockets. The cuttings and Naharro's list I left on the table, but I took the gun. There was a pitcher of water in a basin on a nightstand near the bed. I poured it on him until he sat up and shook his head.

"How did you like the rematch?" I croaked...

PLUNDER
of the SUN

by David Dodge

A HARD CASE CRIME NOVEL

A HARD CASE CRIME BOOK
(HCC-010)
First Hard Case Crime edition: May 2005

Published by

Titan Books
A division of Titan Publishing Group Ltd
144 Southwark Street
London
SE1 0UP

in collaboration with Winterfall LLC

ISBN 978-0-85768-321-2

Design direction by Max Phillips
www.maxphillips.net

The name "Hard Case Crime" and the Hard Case Crime logo are trademarks of Winterfall LLC. Hard Case Crime books are selected and edited by Charles Ardai.

Printed and bound by CPI Group (UK) Ltd, Croydon, CR0 4YY

Visit us on the web at www.HardCaseCrime.com

This is for
LETTIE CONNELL

PLUNDER OF THE SUN

I

The man who had made an appointment to meet me in Santiago's *Parque Forestal* was late getting there, and the sun shining on the bench where I waited made me sleepy. I dozed off, so I didn't hear him coming. When he said, "Mr. Colby?" I opened my eyes and looked up, expecting to see him standing in front of me.

I saw a girl. She was Latin and pretty, with big dark eyes, smooth dark hair, a bright skin and a slim figure. She was wearing white, a kind of nurse's uniform minus the starch, with a white ribbon in her hair instead of a cap. That much I saw before I looked at the man she was pushing in a wheel chair.

He was about fifty, at a guess. He looked ugly and soft and helpless, like a slug. His skin was corpse-gray. His hands, lying on the lap robe spread over his knees, were younger than the rest of him, so he might not have been as old as I thought. I never did find out how old he really was, and it doesn't matter now, to him or to anybody else.

I said, "Señor Berrien?"

"Yes."

I stood up. He said in Spanish, "This is my nurse, Ana Luz."

I said it enchanted me to make her acquaintance, wondering whether her name was Señorita Luz or whether he had introduced her by her first name to show that she was only a servant, the way you would say, "This is Mary Jane, the scullery maid." Nothing in her manner gave me a hint either way. She said *tanto gusto* and swung the wheel chair around so that it faced the bench. After she had arranged Berrien's lap robe, she went to the far end of the bench and sat down. I sat at the near end, next to Berrien.

We talked in English. His was book English, with an accent I couldn't identify except that it sounded more Central European than South American.

"I hope you will excuse me for insisting that we meet in the park," he said. "A wheel chair is easier to manage on a path than in most other places."

"I could have come to see you."

"It wasn't necessary. I visit the park daily for my exercise."

I looked at his shoes, which showed below the lap robe. They were worn.

"I can walk," he said, seeing my eyes move. "I'm not supposed to do any more of it than is necessary to keep my legs functioning."

"Heart?"

"Yes."

That was all, for nearly a minute. He was thinking, trying to make up his mind how to say what he had to say. I kept quiet because it wasn't my turn to talk. I didn't know him from the cow that kicked over the lamp. I didn't know who he was or what he wanted or where he had got my name, only that he called himself Alfredo Berrien and had telephoned me to make an appointment to talk business. He hadn't said what kind of business.

After he had studied the design of his lap robe for a while, he said, "The American consul in Valparaíso told me about you. He says that you are capable and trustworthy, and that your services are available for a proper fee."

He waited for me to say something. When I didn't, he said, "Can you arrange to leave Chile within the next few days?"

"To go where?"

"Peru."

"What do you want done in Peru?"

"Nothing. I want you to carry something there for me."

"Go on."

"There is an American ship, the *Talca*, leaving Valparaíso for the north in three days. I am sailing on her. I want you to be aboard. Before we sail, I will give you a small package which you can put in your pocket. You will keep it until we leave the ship at Callao, where you will return it to me. At that time I will pay you a thousand dollars."

"What's in the package?"

"You won't know."

"It won't be in my pocket, then."

"Not for a thousand dollars?"

"Not for a lot of thousands of dollars. If you feel like telling me what it's all about, I'll listen. Otherwise, the answer is no."

"What if I give you my word that I am not asking you to do anything criminal?"

"I don't know that your word is any good."

He took it as I meant it, without getting his feelings hurt. I said, "And if you're not afraid of trouble, why pay me a thousand dollars?"

He didn't answer the question directly. He had to think again. When I got tired of watching him, I watched his nurse, who was looking at the river.

A breeze twitched the ribbon in her hair. She put up her hand to it. She had small slender hands, the wrists no bigger than a child's. The rest of her was grown-up enough for anybody. She looked about half her patient's age.

Alfredo Berrien picked his words carefully.

"The—object—which I want you to take to Peru is a Peruvian antique. It belongs in Peru, and the Peruvian law was broken when it was taken out of the country. I want to return it there. But the Chilean law also restricts exportation of native antiques, and the Chilean authorities would refuse to recognize the Peruvian origin of the object if they discovered it. It will have to be smuggled."

"Why can I smuggle it any easier than you can?"

He smiled, leaning forward to arrange a loose corner of the lap robe.

"I am a dealer in antiques. They know me here, in Chile. I…"

The smile became a death's-head grin that made his face look like a skull. The gray of his cheeks turned a dirty blue. He made a gasping noise, and rolled his eyes toward his nurse, trying at the same time to get his hand up to his breast pocket.

She beat him to it. He had a handkerchief there, and something small made of glass that she wrapped in the handkerchief and crushed with her fingers before she shoved the handkerchief up against his nose. His eyes, as he struggled to inhale, popped with the effort he was making.

I said, "Shall I try to find a glass of water?"

The nurse didn't answer. I had said it in English, wanting to find out if Berrien was talking that language because it came easier to him than another or because he didn't want her to know what we were talking about. She didn't tumble. I said it again, in Spanish.

"No, gracias." She helped his groping hand up to the handkerchief. "He will be all right in a moment."

The stuff, whatever it was, took hold fast. Berrien's breathing stopped sounding as if it came from a cut throat. The blue faded from his face. Thirty seconds later, when he took the handkerchief away from his nose, there was a little water in his eyes. Otherwise he looked like the same old healthy corpse.

"I'm sorry," he said faintly.

The nurse was taking his pulse—not timing it, but feeling for the thread of life in his arteries to see if he was in shape to go on talking. He lay back in the wheel chair, looking shrunken and dead, his eyes closed, waiting for her to make up his mind. After a moment she put his wrist in his lap, touched him lightly on the shoulder with what might have been an encouraging pat, and went back to her seat at the end of the bench.

When his eyes opened, I said, "Do you get those things very often?"

"Too often. One of them will kill me some day."

"It's not a nice thing to think about."

"I try not to think about it. I keep my mind occupied with other things—such as the matter we were discussing."

He wiped his eyes before he put the handkerchief back in his breast pocket.

"You were asking why it would be easier for you to smuggle the package," he said, as if nothing had happened. "I am a dealer in antiques, well known in all these countries. I and my baggage will be thoroughly searched, both at Valparaíso and at Callao. You, as an American—presumably a tourist—will have no trouble. They will not go through your pockets, even if they bother to search your luggage. You will have a ten-day sea trip and a thousand dollars for enjoying the sea air."

"This antique must be pretty valuable."

He turned his hands palm up in his lap.

"Who can say? What is the value of a rare coin containing two cents worth of copper, for example? Whatever someone wishes to pay for it."

"You're speculating a thousand dollars that it's worth a lot more than that to somebody."

"I speculate every day of my life, Mr. Colby." The lines in his gray face deepened. "Each morning when I awake, I wonder if it is for the last time. Then I put it out of my mind and try to interest myself in other things. There is little pleasure that I can buy with my money, except through using it to surround myself with things of beauty. Sometimes I sell them, sometimes I keep them for what they are. But their value—to me—

is not something that can be measured in terms of the money I will leave behind when I die."

He turned his head toward the nurse as he finished speaking. It may have been only a coincidence, but I wondered. Just then she was a thing of beauty in anybody's language. The breeze had stiffened suddenly, flipping the ribbon in her hair so that she put up both hands to secure it. That particular gesture is one of the most feminine things a woman can do, to my mind. Her back straightens, her breasts push forward, her head comes up, her arms curve like the handles on a Grecian vase. Even a homely woman looks different when she is fixing her hair. Berrien's nurse wasn't homely.

She saw us watching her. I don't know if there was any particular expression in Berrien's face, but there must have been something in mine, because she flushed and dropped her arms. I looked at Berrien again.

"Before I say yes or no, tell me one more thing. What happens to me if I'm caught?"

"You must not be caught. They would confiscate the—object."

"What else?"

"You would be fined, possibly put in jail. But you must not be caught, Mr. Colby. I came to you because I heard that you were a resourceful man. I am counting on your resourcefulness. You *must not* be caught!"

He was trying so hard to sell me the idea that he leaned forward in the wheel chair and raised his voice. The nurse said warningly, *"Cuídese, don Alfredo."*

He relaxed.

"I'm as interested in staying out of jail as you are in keeping your antique," I said. "If it were left to me, I'd take a plane from here. They're a lot easier with inspections at the airport than they are at the *aduana* in Valparaíso."

"No. No. I cannot travel by air, and I want you where I can see what you are doing."

"You think I might run out?"

"If I thought that, I would not have come to you. But if something goes wrong, there may be things I can do to help if I am on hand. You must sail with me on the *Talca*."

It was reasonable enough. I knew a heart case as bad as he was couldn't board a plane, even with an oxygen tank to keep him company. He watched me anxiously while I thought it over.

A thousand dollars was a thousand dollars. I could use it, although I didn't need it so bad that I had to grab it without thinking. And Berrien's deal gave me the nudge I needed to leave Santiago. Once I had thought I would stay in Chile forever, but forever turned out to be about a year. It was time to move along. I knew that I could probably get his package through without trouble. Breaking the law didn't bother me. If his story was halfway on the level—and I believed part of it—the kind of law I was breaking didn't matter much.

I thought about it, sitting there in the hot sunlight with the breeze from the river hitting me in the face, half-decided to tell him that I would need twenty-four hours to think it over. It was the nurse who made up my mind for me.

She got up to rearrange his lap robe, which the breeze had blown loose again. When she had tucked it in, she stood behind the wheel chair instead of going back to her seat, watching my face the way Berrien was watching it. She might not understand English, but she knew what was going on. And she was as anxious to hear my answer as he was.

I said to Berrien, "You don't want me to know any more about this package than you have told me?"

"No. But what I have told you is the truth."

"After you give it to me, what's to stop me from…"

"Your word."

"You don't know me. You haven't any more reason to trust my word than I have to trust yours."

"I know your consul in Valparaíso. I trust his judgment. He says that your word is good."

He meant it as a selling point, to show me that he was a man of honor who could understand honor in others. I wasn't sold. Half the crooks I knew expected everybody else to be crooked, and the other half were smart enough to realize that honesty was useful—in somebody else. I thought Alfredo Berrien was pretty smart.

The nurse was still trying to make something out of my expression. On an impulse, I looked her in the eye and said, "O.K., I'll do it."

Everybody in South America knows what O.K. means. She stopped looking anxious. I couldn't tell whether she was relieved or disappointed.

2

Berrien and I arranged to meet in Valparaíso on the morning of the day the *Talca* sailed. He had already reserved an extra cabin, but he told me he would cancel it so I could book the reservation in my own name. He didn't want anything in the record to connect us.

At the ticket office I learned that the *Talca* was a freighter, with eight cabins on the boat deck. The one I got—Berrien's cancellation—was the only one open. I had my passport stamped with a Peruvian tourist visa and spent the next couple of days cleaning up the bills I owed around town and clearing myself with the authorities. On the morning of the third day, I went down to Valparaíso on the train.

The consul there was a friend of mine. I stopped in to see him before I kept my date with Berrien.

"What do you know about Alfredo Berrien?" I asked him.

"Who's he?"

"A heart case in a wheel chair, with a good-looking nurse."

"Oh, him. Nothing much. He had a letter of introduction. He wanted the name of some unattached American he could hire to do what he called an unusual job. You were the only man I knew of in Chile who did unusual jobs, so I sent him along."

"You never met him before he brought the letter of introduction?"

"Never even heard of him."

"He said he wanted to hire me because you had recommended me, and he trusted your judgment."

"Why shouldn't he?"

"No reason. No reason why he should, either."

"You're just suspicious by nature. What was the job?"

"Smuggling."

His eyebrows went up. He said, "I see what you mean. Did you accept?"

"If I don't tell you, you won't have to worry about it. I'm leaving Chile for Peru, and my mail will come here. Hold it until you hear from me."

"If you get into trouble in Peru, you're on your own, you know. There's nothing the consular service can do to help you."

"I know. Thanks for the recommendation, anyway."

Half an hour later I met Berrien in the Plaza Sotomayor. The package was in his lap. He handed it to me as Ana Luz wheeled him by the bench where I was reading a newspaper. I went on reading until they had time to cross the plaza, then looked at the package.

It was about the size of a small book, wrapped in brown paper and lumped over with gobs of red sealing-wax that had been stamped down with a signet ring or a cameo. The imprint was a tiny llama, ears and tail up, very finely cut. Berrien's confidence in my word didn't prevent him from seeing to it that I wasn't tempted to get nosy.

I didn't care what he thought. What I wanted to know was whether he had hired me because he was really afraid of being searched at the *aduana* or for some other reason.

I went down to the *aduana* early. The customs inspectors didn't waste two minutes on me. I had the package in my inside coat pocket—I had to cut the lining to squeeze it in—but I could just as well have wrapped it in a shirt and put it in my bag, because they gave the bag the fast one-two-three that American tourists get in any country where people who have dollars to spend are popular. They asked me the usual questions about firearms, jewelry, and silver. I said I didn't have any. That was all there was to it.

I was sitting in a quiet corner of the *aduana* when Berrien and Ana Luz showed up. They had four bags with them, and a small box that Berrien declared for duty. The box held odds and ends of jewelry, a gold *florero*, a piece of carved jade, other junk the inspectors had to take out and weigh and argue about. But Berrien got it through, for a price. Then the inspectors went at his bags.

It was a real job, this time. They took everything out, unfolded clothes, shook them, peered at the lining of the bags, and tapped things to see if they sounded hollower than they should. Ana Luz's baggage got the same treatment. The inspectors had more sport with her than with Berrien, because she owned some pretty fancy underwear. They held things up to the light and made a game out of looking for something concealed in the frills. But even with the horseplay, it was easy to see they meant business. When they finished with the bags, they wheeled Berrien off to a side room for the personal treatment. Ana Luz and a matron went into another room.

Ana Luz was the first one to come back. She looked so stiff and uncomfortable that I couldn't help smiling. It was bad luck that she happened to see me then, because she turned a bright, angry pink. I was sorry about the smile. It's humiliating enough to be stripped to the skin and peered at by strangers without having other strangers laugh at you. It was the second time I had made her blush, without meaning to either time.

Berrien came back from the search looking the same as ever, ready for burial. Ana Luz wheeled him through the *aduana* and out to the pier where the *Talca* was tied up. I followed along.

They hoisted Berrien and his wheel chair up to the boat deck with a winch. The nurse and I had to climb the gangplank and a couple of ladders to get there, dodging cables most of the way. The ship had finished working cargo, and stevedores were already lowering the strongbacks into place in the hatches. An hour later we put to sea.

The *Talca* didn't have much in the way of passenger accommodations, just the cabins on the boat deck and a few steamer chairs cluttering the deck between the cabins and the lifeboats. Passengers were supposed to eat with the officers. Berrien couldn't make it up and down the ladder to the messroom, which was on the main deck, so he and Ana Luz had their meals in his cabin. I met the other passengers at dinner the first night out.

Three of them were North Americans, two men and a woman. The men had *gringo* written all over them. I don't know just what it is about North Americans, but you can tell them a mile off, wherever you meet them and whatever language they happen to be talking. There's something in the way they carry themselves. These two had it. One said he was a traveling salesman for a United States manufacturer of pressure-cookers. I forget his name, but a traveling salesman is a traveling salesman, whether you find him kicking around South America or in a country store in Kansas. He told jokes in three languages, played poker with me and the ship's officers, and called the captain by his first name inside of two days. The other man was a big, rangy, hard-faced fellow who looked as if he could have played pro football for a living at one time. He didn't say what his business was. His name was Jefferson, Jeff to the traveling salesman first and to the rest of us later. He played good poker, a little loose but not reckless, and didn't talk much.

The *gringa* was a young blonde piece making a tour of South America on her own. She painted her mouth square at the corners, like a comic-strip glamor girl. She didn't speak any Spanish and didn't have to, because there would always be some guy hanging around to translate for her. During the first day out she had the third officer showing her how to weave a string belt. He had to put his arms around her from behind to manage the strings, and she did everything she could, short of biting his ear, to make him realize he was holding something real nice. She was that type. Her name was Julie.

The other passengers were a middle-aged Peruvian

official of some kind and his wife, both fat and con-
tented with each other, and a tall beaknosed Englishman
named Harris who said Good morning, Good afternoon
and Good evening once a day each. It was just an
average passenger list—on the surface. I found out that
something was going on beneath the surface when
Berrien learned that Jeff was aboard.

Berrien had another attack just after reaching the
ship, and stayed in his cabin during the first two days at
sea. He had a hand bell that he rang when he wanted
Ana Luz, so she could spend her time outside in the sun
on the boat deck and still be within call. Jeff paid her a
lot of attention. He spoke easy Spanish, and Julie the
dizzy blonde kept the other unoccupied males from
giving him any competition. She tried to add Jeff to her
string as well. He wouldn't play—with her. But any time
Ana Luz was on deck, Jeff was pretty sure to show up.
She didn't encourage him or discourage him. He was
there just the same.

On the third afternoon, he came up to the boat deck
after lunch and took one of the steamer chairs near
Berrien's cabin. He was waiting for Ana Luz to show
after she had snugged Berrien down for his afternoon
nap. This time Berrien himself came out of the cabin,
walking, holding Ana Luz's arm and taking slow, careful
steps. He saw me first—I was leaning against one of the
lifeboats—and then Jeff. He stopped dead.

I thought he was going to have another attack. Ana
Luz, who was watching his feet, looked up quickly at his
face, then at Jeff. She was puzzled, Berrien was scared.
That was all I could make out of their expressions

during the few seconds before Jeff said, "*¿Qué tal, Alfredo? ¿Como estás?*"

"*Bien, gracias.*" Berrien had recovered himself, although his face was grayer than usual. "*¿Como estás tu?*"

"*Bien.*"

Berrien began to walk again, carefully putting one foot in front of the other until he and Ana Luz had rounded the corner of the far cabin and were out of sight.

I said to Jeff, "Who's your friend?"

"His name is Berrien."

"He looks like a sick man."

"He is—the crook!"

Jeff hauled his long frame up out of the deck chair and went down the ladder to the main deck so he wouldn't have to talk any more. I would have liked to know what it was in particular that made him think Berrien was a crook, and where he had known him well enough so that they used the Spanish "thou" to each other.

Berrien and Ana Luz came around the other end of the cabins, starting a second lap. The Peruvian couple, the Englishman, Julie and the salesman were digesting their lunches in steamer chairs ranged along the cabin bulkhead, the Peruvians dozing, the Englishman and the salesman looking at Julie's legs. She had her skirts up too high and was pretending to be asleep, all innocence. If she had pulled her skirts down, they would all have gone to sleep and Berrien could have passed me the message he wanted to give me. As it was, he moved his head an inch in the direction of his cabin the second time he shuffled by.

There was nothing I could do about it until dinner time. I stalled until everybody else had gone down to the messroom, then ducked into his cabin.

He was sitting up in the wheel chair. Ana Luz was reading poetry to him, her voice low and soothing. It was the formal Spanish verse that is all meter and no rhyme, like waves in a pond. His eyes were closed. She was reading:

Para mi corazón basta tu pecho
Para tu libertad bastan mis alas
Desde mi boca llegará hasta el cielo
Lo que estaba dormido sobre tu alma.

She finished the verse before she put the book down. I wondered whose idea it had been to pick that particular poem for a nurse to read to a hopeless invalid. It translates this way, more or less:

For my heart, thy breast is enough
For thy liberty, my wings are enough
From my mouth, that which has slept on thy soul
Will arise to the sky.

Berrien opened his eyes when she stopped reading.

I said, "*¿Que quiere?*"

"Speak English." He looked worried. "Where is the package?"

"In a place where nobody will be able to get it."

"Are you sure?"

I was as sure as anybody would feel with the thing digging a hole into his armpit, but I only said Yes.

"Good. You will have to be very careful with it. There is a man aboard the ship who would do anything to get it."

"Jefferson?"

"How did you know?"

"You jumped when you saw him."

"I am afraid of him. He would stop at nothing to get it away from me. Nothing."

"He doesn't look like a collector of antiques."

"He is a thief. He would steal anything that could be sold."

"Does he know what you have?"

"He knows or suspects. He has been trying to get information from Ana Luz."

"How much information does she have to give him?"

"What do you mean?"

"Does she know what it is, or how much it's worth, or anything else about it?"

"Of course not." He was surprised at the question. "She only knows that you are carrying a package for me, and that we must all be discreet."

"Do you talk English with me because you don't trust her?"

"I have no reason to distrust her. I talk English with you because I am a cautious man by nature. But you need have no worry on her account."

"She doesn't understand English?"

"No."

All this time Ana Luz had been pretending to read poetry. Her eyes hadn't moved once. If she wasn't able to make any sense out of what we were saying, she was trying hard.

I said, "Thanks for the tip. I'll be careful."

"I am counting on you, Mr. Colby."

"Don't worry."

I went down to dinner.

Afterwards Jeff, the salesman, the Englishman, the radio operator, the skipper and I played poker until midnight. Jeff was glum and reckless. He lost a couple of big pots on bluffs that didn't work, and won a couple of bigger pots on what I thought were bluffs but didn't have enough cards to investigate. His kind of play made the game too rich for my blood. At midnight, the radio operator and I gave up our seats to the steward and the first officer.

I had a last cigarette with the radio operator on the boat deck. He was a chunky, friendly man, an ex-navy brass-pounder. He said he had a bottle in his cabin if I felt like a small one before turning in.

"Thanks, no, Sparks. I'm tired. Some other time."

"Me, too." He yawned until his jaws cracked. "I've got to roll out at four A.M. to work traffic. Me for the sack."

We said good night. He went to the radio shack. I went to my cabin.

Fifteen minutes later, after I had crawled into my bunk with the package tucked under my pillow, the radio key began clattering.

I had the after cabin on the port side, right around the corner from the radio shack, so Sparks' fist was practically in my ear. It didn't bother me. I was already in that half-conscious state where you start dreaming before you are really asleep. I was back in the army, a headset over my ears, sitting around in a circle with half a dozen other buck privates while the Signal Corps sergeant in the middle of the circle tapped out practice messages to us on a buzzer. He was a brute, that sergeant. He thought anybody who couldn't take forty words a minute ought to be on permanent K.P. Right in the middle of a message to one man, he'd break in with the next man's name and start a new message, hoping to catch somebody asleep. You had to be on your toes, listening for your name to pop into the middle of a sentence. He was sending something to the man across the circle from me when the buzzer said C-O-L-B-Y.

I grabbed my pencil and pad, but it was no use. He was sending too fast. I couldn't make head or tail of the message. He bared his teeth at me over the key, his big ham of a hand beating away like a riveting gun, faster and faster, nothing but a blurred buzz of sound in the head-set, and I thought: Another week of K.P. for you, Al. You're in the Army now, you're not behind a plow, you'll never get rich…

I snapped awake. The key was still going. I jumped out of my bunk and ran to the bulkhead that was the partition between my cabin and the radio shack. The sound was fainter there. It was better at the porthole, but not good enough. By the time I got into a pair of pants, the key had stopped.

From the doorway of my cabin, it was easy to muscle up onto the roof of the superstructure. There was a bright moon. The snowy peaks of the Andes, a hundred miles from the coast along which we were sailing, were like a bridge of clouds across the horizon, but I didn't waste any time on the view. I could see the whole ship aft of the bridge. The only movement I could make out was the lookout on the bridge wing, sneaking a smoke. I walked all around the edge of the superstructure, looking for a reflection of light from the cabins below. They were all dark, except for the radio shack.

When I finished my round, I squatted down by the water tank on top of the radio shack and waited for somebody to come out of the door below. Nobody did. There were no more messages. The antenna lead-in coming up through the roof stopped humming when Sparks shut off the power. I heard him knocking around down below for a couple of minutes, and then his light went off.

My feet were bare, so I didn't make any noise dropping to the deck. I whispered "Sparks!" through his porthole.

His bunk creaked. "Who is it?"

"Colby."

"What do you want?"

"The drink."

His light went on. He got out of the bunk to open the door. He looked surprised when he saw me there in nothing but a pair of pants, but he let me in and reached for the bottle under his bunk.

I said, "What I really want is to know what was in the message you just sent."

He filled two shot-glasses with whiskey, held them at

eye-level to see that they were equal, and handed me one.

"None of your business. *Salud*."

"*Salud*. If it wasn't my business, I wouldn't be asking."

"Then the rule book says I can't tell you. Have another?"

"One is enough for me. How much would it cost to have you forget the rule book for a couple of minutes?"

He smiled at me—with his mouth, not his eyes.

"You don't try to bribe a man when you're drinking his whiskey, laddie. Go back to bed."

"Tell me who sent the message, then."

"The rule book says no."

"Was it ship's business or a private message?"

"The rule book covers that, too."

"Was it a man or a woman?"

He poured himself a second drink before he answered.

"What's it to you?"

"My name was in it."

"You read code?"

"I read enough to recognize my own name. I didn't get any of the rest of it, and I'm interested."

"It could have been ship's business. The passenger list, maybe."

"I thought you worked your traffic at four A.M."

"I didn't say it *was* ship's business. I said it could have been. Now go to bed and let me sleep, laddie."

It was no use trying to get anything out of him. The rule book was a lot more important to him than I was. I thanked him for the drink and went back to my cabin. I didn't even think of the damn package until I got back in my bunk and found it still there under my pillow, where anybody could have pinched it while I was out prowling around.

Lying in the dark, I checked over the probabilities. If the message had been ship's business, it didn't interest me. But I didn't think that Sparks would have stayed awake to transmit ship's business at midnight unless it was an emergency, and I couldn't think of an emergency that would involve me except the boilers blowing up. If it was private business, one of the passengers had been so anxious to get a message off that night that he—or she—had waited up until Sparks left the poker game, and talked him into sending it *inmediatamente.* Counting out the poker players we had left below—I could find out in the morning if anybody had quit the game within a couple of minutes after we did—it left the Peruvian couple, Julie, Ana Luz, and Berrien.

Before I went to sleep, I plastered the package to my ribs with enough adhesive tape so that anybody who wanted it would have to take me with it.

3

Nobody had quit the poker game until three o'clock. I learned that from Jeff, who had won a potful of money, mostly from Harris, the Englishman. My list still included only four names.

Julie cornered me after breakfast. The salesman was tagging her, but she got rid of him by asking him to bring a sweater from her cabin. As soon as he left us, she stuck out her lip at me and looked sly.

"What were you doing up on the roof last night?"

"Where were you?"

"Looking at the moon from a deck chair."

"Anybody with you?"

"The mate—the cute one."

"Did he see me?"

"He was too busy. What were you doing?"

"Getting my exercise."

"It's a funny way to get exercise. But I like the way you look with your shirt off." She ran a red, sharply pointed fingernail up my forearm. "Nice muscles."

"The third mate has nice muscles, too. Did you tell him that you saw me?"

"I haven't told anybody—yet. You're kind of a mystery man, aren't you? I like mystery men."

"That's good. Did you happen to see anybody go in or come out of the radio shack just before you saw me?"

"I couldn't see the radio shack. All I saw were those beautiful muscles in the moonlight." She looked at me from the corners of her eyes. "Where are you taking them, mystery man?"

"Why do you want to know?"

"I was just thinking that you might be going to Lima. I'm going to be in Lima in about a week, after I go up to Cuzco and poke around a lot of moldy old Inca ruins. I might let you take me out, some time."

"I'd like that."

She nodded solemnly. "But you'll have to tell me what you were doing up on the roof."

"What if I don't?"

"I might tell somebody about it."

"Go right ahead."

She was disappointed. The salesman came back with her sweater before she could say any more.

She was probably just what she seemed to be, but I didn't cross her off my list until she left the ship at Mollendo to take the train to Arequipa, a hundred miles up in the *sierra* on the way to Cuzco. The salesman decided that he had business in Arequipa and left with her, although his ticket was good to Callao.

We were fourteen hours in Mollendo unloading cargo. Everybody went ashore except Berrien and Ana Luz. Berrien couldn't have gone ashore even if he had wanted to, because Mollendo is a shallow-water port, the second best in Peru and one of the worst in the world. Ships have to anchor half a mile off shore and unload into lighters. Passengers are taken off in a launch. From the launch you go ashore by way of a bos'n's chair on a cable let down by a donkey engine on the pier. The launch rocks a lot, and the chair kicks you two or three times in the seat of the pants while you are fitting yourself into it. After you reach dry land, there is a stiff climb—too stiff for a wheel chair—up a cliff to the town. And after you get to the top, it isn't worth it anyway.

I went ashore only because I knew the West Coast Cable agent there. We had lunch together. During lunch I asked him questions about the rules covering privacy of radio messages transmitted from vessels at sea. He said they were pretty strict, and read me part of the International Convention. I could see that my chances of getting anything out of Sparks were hopeless, unless I wanted to try a bribe bigger than I could afford. I would just have to wait and see how the cards fell.

After lunch I wandered around town, killing time. It was March, late summer and hotter than the top of a stove. I walked four blocks uphill, two blocks over, and came back. That was Mollendo. Beer seemed like a good idea by the time I finished the *gran tour,* so I stopped at a *cantina* to cool off.

Jeff was there, alone, breaking matchsticks between his fingers and dropping them into an ash tray. He didn't say anything when I sat down at his table, only nodded. When my beer came, he picked up his own glass and drank to keep me company, then went on breaking matchsticks.

Five minutes later he said, "Hot."

"Too hot."

"Some dump, Mollendo."

"I've seen better. What are you doing ashore?"

"Stretching my legs."

"Lost interest in the nurse?"

He grunted. I knew that Ana Luz didn't mean a thing to him after Berrien learned that he was trying to pump her, but I wanted to try him out. He said half-heartedly, "Maybe I ought to go back to the ship and see how she's getting along."

"I'll split the cost of the launch with you."

We finished our beer and started down the dusty street.

Right at the foot of the street, just before it turned into a steep cobblestoned fire-escape going down the cliff, there was a tourist trap, a *tienda* full of junk silver, alpaca rugs, carved wooden souvenirs, Indian weaving, the same stuff you find in the same kind of shops all over the world. As we went by, I looked at the rugs on display. Anybody would have looked at them. They were fur patchwork, black and brown and white alpaca skins cut up into little pieces, triangular, square, oval, any shape, all sewn together into the ugliest designs you could think up if you worked hard at it for a month. I wouldn't have had one of the things if it had been lined with dollar bills. But Jeff caught my arm.

"Wait a minute."

It wasn't the rugs that interested him. He was looking at a little silver pot in the window, a squat tarnished thing about four inches high with animal figures hammered into the metal. He studied it for about thirty seconds, all the time holding my arm. Then he turned me around and pushed me toward the doorway of the *tienda*.

"Buy a rug."

"I don't want a rug."

"Bargain with the guy anyway. Offer him half of what he asks, and put up a fight, but let him stick you. I'll pay."

It was nothing to me if he wanted to waste his money, and I was curious. We went into the store.

The rug cost three hundred *soles,* about twenty dollars American, twice what it was worth even to somebody who wanted it. The storekeeper and I spent fifteen minutes arguing about it. All that time Jeff wandered around the store fingering things and asking prices. While the storekeeper was bundling up the rug, Jeff planked a silver *copa* down on the counter—not the pot, but a shinier piece he had lifted out of the window.

"How much?"

"Five hundred *soles.*"

"*Por dios,* what do you take me for, a tourist? Two hundred."

"I regret it deeply, señor. The silver is *precio fijo.*"

"In that case, it remains yours."

Jeff turned away.

The storekeeper forgot about his fixed prices and came down a hundred *soles.* Jeff went up fifty. The storekeeper came down fifty. They stuck there. Jeff put the *copa* back in the window and picked up another one—still not the pot. They couldn't reach a price on the second piece, either. Jeff was keeping his bids low, feeling the storekeeper out to see just how much he would come down from his opening price to make a sale. I had played poker with him, so I recognized the technique.

When he finally got around to the pot, the storekeeper opened with eight hundred *soles*—a higher price than the others because the pot was a real *antigua,* genuine native manufacture, heavy silver, and so on. Jeff got it for five hundred.

Going down the hill, he gave me back my money.

The boatman who took us out to the *Talca* got the rug for a tip. While we bounced along in the launch, the wind whipping salt spray into our faces from the tops of the waves, Jeff tapped the silver pot with his finger.

"Know what it's worth?"

I took it from him and looked at it. It was old and heavy. That was all I could make out of it.

"More than you paid for it," I said.

"About five hundred dollars. It's pre-Conquest by two hundred years. I could sell it to that old thief Berrien for seven thousand *soles* right now."

More than I wanted to find out how a *gringo* who looked like an ex-football player had learned to pick a six-hundred-year-old piece of Inca silver out of a collection of tourist souvenirs in a store window, I wanted to know what his grudge was. I said, "What have you got against Berrien?"

He studied the pot for a minute, rolling it between his hands.

"Not a thing," he said shortly.

We didn't talk any more about it, and he didn't pay any attention to Ana Luz after we were aboard.

There was a new passenger on the *Talca* when we hoisted anchor that evening. He was *peruano*, a young fellow down from Arequipa on the train to go to Lima by boat because he had a bad heart and couldn't fly there. He told us all about himself at dinner. He said his name was Raul Cornejo. His English was good, his clothes were good, his fingernails were clean. He looked pretty healthy to have a bad heart. And I wondered what difference it made to a heart whether you dropped seventy-five hundred feet with it to sea level in three hours by plane to Lima, or in four hours and a half by train to Mollendo.

People with bad hearts were beginning to make me suspicious. That unexplained radio message with my name in it had got under my skin. Only Berrien and Ana Luz knew—or ought to know—that I was anything but a tourist. If one of them was double-crossing me for some reason, I had plenty to worry about. I still had to go through customs at Callao. If the radio message had been a tip-off that I was smuggling something, I would land in the can in a hurry. I didn't think it had been a tip-off, because I couldn't see any sense to a tip-off, but I didn't know what was going on. I had to figure on all possibilities. My hunch was that somebody—I didn't have any favorites—would be making a try for the package before the *Talca* reached Callao. The break would have to come within thirty-six hours, the *Talca's* running time between Mollendo and Callao.

The thirty-six hours covered two nights and a day. The first night, I left the poker game early, about ten. I told everybody within earshot, including the captain, Sparks, the first officer, Harris, Jeff and the steward, that I was going right to bed. I didn't tell them I was getting jumpy and wanted the action to start if it was going to start, but I hoped somebody would get the idea.

There were two ladders leading up to the boat deck, port and starboard. I went up the starboard ladder because the ship rolled that way as I came out of the messroom, sending me down the slanting deck. When I reached the top of the ladder—or when my head and shoulders reached the top of the ladder—I saw Ana Luz and the young *peruano* who called himself Raul Cornejo standing in the nook between two lifeboats, talking.

I stopped where I was. The moonlight was bright on their faces. I knew right away they weren't just chatting about how many knots the *Talca* might be making. They were talking business—angry business. I hung there on the ladder, not moving, hoping that my coat wouldn't flap in the wind and give me away, trying to catch the conversation. They were both talking at once, their voices low and hot, and I couldn't get it. It didn't last long, anyway. In the middle of it, he lifted his hand and smacked her.

It was a good stiff slap, right on the mouth. It turned her head in my direction. She was looking at me, her face still twisted from the blow, when his hand came back, knuckle side this time, whanged her head the other way, then back with the palm to turn her face toward me again, crack, crack, crack.

"*¡Cállate!*" he hissed at her. "*¡Ya hablo yo! Tu vas a…*"

He didn't have time to tell her what she was going to do. I think if she hadn't seen me there I might have been able to check my gentlemanly impulses long enough to try to hear more of what he had to say to her. But you can't stand still when a lady has her face slapped while she is looking at you, whoever she is.

I got to him before he knew I was there. He was small and light-boned. I jammed him back against a lifeboat, my left hand on his chest, and whacked him three times the way he had whacked Ana Luz, only with more steam behind it. It almost put him to sleep, not quite. His hand went under his coat, pushing against mine, trying to get to his armpit. I shifted my hand ahead of his and felt the gun.

I didn't know what to do. As long as it was just a little friendly face-slapping, I could be another crazy *gringo* who objected to seeing ladies pushed around, and no hard feelings. But if I took his gun away from him, I made a personal feud out of it. And if I didn't take his gun away from him, he was going to get at it sooner or later and let me have the business. He squirmed like an eel, trying to get out from under my hand. He wasn't afraid, or badly hurt. He just wanted to kill me.

While I held him there, trying to make up my mind what to do with him, Ana Luz said warningly, "Raul!"

It reached him. He kept struggling, but the hell-fire began to leave his face. He took his hand out from under his lapel and used it to pull at my wrist, as if that had been all he was trying to do all the time. I let him work free.

"It is a bad thing to strike a lady, *caballero,*" I said.

He kept his eyes down and his mouth shut, breathing hard, fighting himself, holding it in while his fingers itched to grab for the gun. I waited another thirty seconds, more to let him calm down than anything else—I wouldn't have liked a bullet in the back any better than in the belly—and then turned to Ana Luz.

"May I take you to your cabin, señorita?"

"Thank you, no. I am perfectly all right."

She made no move. I said, "Shall I leave you here?"

"Please."

Her face, in the moonlight, still showed the marks of fingers, dark on white. I supposed that he would smack her again after I got out of sight, but there wasn't anything I could do about it. I left them standing by the lifeboats and went to my cabin.

Nothing else happened that night, except that I picked Raul as a good man to keep my eye on. If he knew Ana Luz well enough to slap her around and say, "Shut up, thou!" to her, he knew her well enough to receive a radio message from her if she had sent one, on her own hook or at Berrien's orders. Berrien was afraid of Jeff and worried about his package. He might have called for reinforcements, either to make sure that I turned the package over to him when I was supposed to, or to make sure that Jeff didn't get it. Or Ana Luz might have ideas about the package herself, and needed help to get it from me. Or everybody aboard the ship might be in cahoots with a band of fanatical Tibetan monks who had sworn to recover the stolen idol's eye I was carrying around taped to my skin. One explanation was no sillier than another.

Nobody tried to crawl through my porthole that night. Berrien took another walk around the deck in the morning, and gave me the nod. I slipped into his cabin at lunchtime, when the boat deck was clear.

Ana Luz was setting out his lunch on the table. There weren't any marks on her face. She didn't look at me when she said *buenos días*.

Berrien was more worried than ever. He said, "You must be very careful today and tonight, Mr. Colby. I am sure that an attempt will be made to steal the package before we land. If there have been no attempts so far, it only means that—they—have been waiting until the last moment to make their escape from the ship easier."

"By 'they,' do you mean Jefferson?"

He hesitated, then nodded.

"Why worry about him? He doesn't even know I have it. Or does he?"

"I don't know. He is a clever and unscrupulous man. He may know more than we think."

"How would he find out?"

"I don't know. I am only warning you to be very careful."

"If you'd tell me something about him—why you are afraid of him, and what…"

"No." Berrien's mouth closed tight on the word. "It is enough to say that he is dangerous."

"Are you afraid of anyone else aboard the ship?"

"No."

"Do you know a *peruano* who calls himself Raul Cornejo?"

Ana Luz was still arranging cutlery. The knives and forks stopped clinking when she heard the name. There wasn't a movement or a sound in the cabin for that one split second, nothing but the steady roll of the ship and the faint vibration carried up through the ship's structure from the engines down below.

"No," Berrien said. "Who is he?"

"Somebody who came aboard at Mollendo. A young fellow. Speaks good English."

"I don't know him."

44

I meant to follow it up. I meant to tell him that Cornejo knew his nurse well enough to slap her around in an argument, and see if he wanted to make a connection between that and a radio message about me that somebody had sent from the ship. But I looked at Ana Luz and knew from her expression that she was ready for me. She had her story.

It wouldn't hurt to wait a little longer, see if I could get something more tangible to go on. I said to Berrien, "All right. I wanted to be sure he wasn't a joker. Is there anything else you want to tell me?"

"Only to be very, very careful."

Ana Luz laid down a fork as I left the cabin. I hoped that I had puzzled her as much as she was puzzling me.

The afternoon dragged by. I sat with Sparks in the radio shack most of the time, listening to record music from the big *radiodifusora* in Lima. We were getting close by then, and the music came in good. Once I asked Sparks if the radio message he had sent had been addressed to somebody in Arequipa. He said I could guess if I wanted to, laddie, and gave me a drink out of his bottle to show that there was nothing personal in his refusal to talk.

I took only one drink. I didn't want to slow my reflexes.

That night we played poker for the last time. Everybody except Harris was leaving the ship at Callao, so we had an open game, the losers trying to get their money back, the winners after a last killing. The only passengers who didn't sit in, except for Berrien and Ana Luz, where the fat Peruvian couple, who always went to bed right after dinner. Sparks and the captain represented the home team, trying to catch Jeff bluffing out on a limb. Raul, who was in the game for the first time, played his cards tight and was careful not to meet my eyes. We called each other "Señor" whenever it was necessary, and didn't say much else. He had a split lip.

At one A.M. I was out three hundred *soles*, all I had in my pocket. Harris was clean, too. Jeff held most of the money. I had intended to stay up all night, figuring I would be less open to trouble if I had company around me until the time came to go ashore, but when I found I couldn't cash a traveler's check without taking all the money in the game—I had nothing but hundreds, in dollars—I decided to quit.

Raul surprised me by offering to stake me. I turned him down. I was tired, and I had begun to think that Berrien's worries about his package were all in his head. Jeff and Raul, the two logical suspects if a play for it was going to be made, sat there as happy as a couple of clams in a bowl of milk, nothing on their minds but the cards. When Harris left the game, I went with him.

We walked out of the messroom together. We hadn't reached the ladder to the boat deck when Raul came through the door behind us.

"Señor Colby!"

We both stopped. Raul came up to me.

"May I have a few words with you?"

"Sure."

Raul looked at Harris. Harris said, "Oh, ah, excuse me, then. Think I'll pop off to bed. 'Night, all."

He went on up the ladder.

Raul motioned toward the side of the ship. We walked over to the railing. The hull wave boiled and hissed below us, greenish white in the glow of the ship's lights. The roll of the ship was more pronounced there than amidships. If a man—even a little man—got a sucker with his back to the rail, and timed the heave just right, it wouldn't be hard to help the sucker overboard.

He didn't try to get me with my back to the rail. He said stiffly, "I wish to make an explanation and an apology for my actions last night."

"Go ahead."

"They were inexcusable. You were perfectly justified in what you did."

"I'm glad you think so."

"You are probably wondering what my relationship is with the lady. She is a member of my family, a distant cousin."

"Yes?"

"Yes. We quarreled about a family matter that would not interest you." (I thought: The hell you say!) "I let my temper carry me away. I am glad to say that she has accepted my apologies. The incident is closed."

It should have been closed, anyway. But he kept it open for another five minutes, bumbling on about his temper and the angry blood of the Cornejos, using a lot of words to say nothing important. I thought he was trying to get up courage to reach for his gun, and I watched his hands. I was going to break his arm if he moved it suddenly.

He didn't try anything, just kept on talking. I finally told him that I was satisfied if he was, and to forget it. I wanted to go to bed. He thought we ought to have a drink together first, to cement the good-neighbor policy. I said any other time, *con mucho gusto,* but not then, and finally pushed him off.

He went back to the messroom. I climbed the ladder to the boat deck, wondering what it was all about. He wasn't the type to apologize to a man who had given him a split lip.

Not ten minutes later I was taking off my shoes in my cabin, yawning, when somebody knocked on the door. I opened the door, ready for anything and anybody. It was Harris, the last person I would have expected. He blinked at the light, the way a man does when he has been outside in the dark for some time and his eyes aren't adjusted to a sudden glare.

"Oh, ah, sorry to knock you up, Colby. May I come in for a minute?"

I let him in. He didn't sit down, just stood there, still blinking, looking embarrassed.

"None of my business, of course," he said uncomfortably. "Don't like to interfere and all that. Supposed I should, really. Been tryin' to make up my mind."

"Trying to make up your mind about what?"

"To tell you that someone was in your cabin."

"When?"

"Few minutes back. Just after we left the poker game. I was standin' behind one of the lifeboats, gulpin' fresh air to get the smoke out of my lungs, when I heard a cabin door close. I turned around in time to see somebody pop around the corner here and beetle off to the other side of the ship. Couldn't say who it was, really, but I doubted that the steward would be messin' around in your cabin at this time of night. Thought I ought to tell you."

"Are you sure it was my cabin?"

"Not positive, of course. Didn't see which door it was. But there are only three cabins on this side; yours, mine, and an empty since that blonde bit of fluff left us at Mollendo. Hardly any reason to steal anything from the empty cabin, and whoever it was wouldn't have time to reach this corner from my cabin before I turned around. Anyone runnin' for cover would be rather stupid to dash for the far corner instead of the near one in any event, don't you think?"

He wasn't as dumb as he looked, the Englishman. Even if I hadn't had plenty of reason to suspect that my cabin would be the one of most interest, I would have agreed with his reasoning.

"Was it a man or a woman?"

"Couldn't say, really. Only caught a glimpse of a moving figure. Thing to do is see if anything is missing and then have the ship searched."

"I'll do that. Thanks for letting me know."

"Not at all, old boy. Not at all. Hope you haven't lost anything valuable."

He backed out of the cabin, apologizing again for interferin' and all that, as if he had stepped on my toes instead of doing me a favor.

It didn't take me long to case the cabin. I wouldn't have noticed anything ordinarily, but with something to look for, I found it. There was a snap on my shaving kit that took a strong thumb to close. I always closed it. It wasn't closed now. There were a few other indications, here and there.

I left the cabin and walked forward, past the empty cabin, past Harris' cabin, and around the corner of the superstructure. Jeff and Raul had the two midship cabins facing forward. The portholes glowed behind their curtains. Lights were still on in the messroom down below, but if the poker game was still going, I couldn't hear it.

I turned a second corner and went aft on the starboard side. The portholes of the Peruvian couple's cabin were dark. So were Berrien's, the middle cabin. So were Ana Luz's, the last cabin aft, opposite mine on the far side of the radio shack.

I knocked on her door. There was no answer right away. I waited, without knocking again. She finally said, "¿Quién es?"

"Colby."

"What do you want?"

"To enter."

The light went on. I heard the hook click—the cabin doors locked from the inside, although not from the outside—and pushed the door open before she had a chance to drop the other hook, the long one you used when you wanted ventilation, into its catch, which would have left me talking through a six-inch crack.

She wore a heavy bathrobe that reached to her ankles. The collar was pulled tightly around her neck. Her hair was down, long over her shoulders. She had taken her makeup off, and her bare feet were in slippers—high-heeled slippers with pompoms on the insteps. They didn't match the shapeless bathrobe.

She said again, "What do you want?"

I went over to the wardrobe against the far bulkhead and opened it. Hanging with her other clothes was a nightgown, one of the frilly things the customs inspectors had sported with, and a negligee that matched her slippers. I closed the wardrobe.

"The first thing I want is to see what you wear under that robe."

She turned pale. I was going to be in a bad spot if I had guessed wrong, but I grabbed her with one arm and stripped the bathrobe down from her shoulder while she kicked at me with her pompoms and stabbed for my eyes with two stiff fingers. She missed, luckily. I wondered where she had learned street-fighting.

She was fully dressed under the bathrobe. I let her go.

"You searched my cabin tonight."

"*¡Tontería!*" She wasn't pale now. Her eyes flashed murder.

"You and Berrien are the only persons who know I have it, unless you told somebody else. He wouldn't tell anyone, and he couldn't search for it himself even if he wanted to. You had Cornejo delay me below while you were in my cabin."

"Madness! I had no reason to go to your cabin."

"Except that you wanted the package. I think you sent a message to Cornejo calling for his help to get it away from me, and decided that you would first search my cabin before you tried to search me."

"You break into my room in the middle of the night to tell me such nonsense?"

She looked pretty scornful and pretty sure of herself standing there, even with the white dress under her bathrobe to give her away. I said, "Let's go see Berrien, then, just as you are. Explain to him why you are dressed so, with your hair and feet so, to make it appear that you had been in bed when you did not have time to take off your clothes. Let's see if he will believe your story."

"Señor Berrien is asleep. You can make your foolish accusations to him in the morning."

"We will wake him. I want him to see you as you are."

"I have given him a sleeping drug. He will not awaken until morning."

"We will see."

I took her by the arm.

She went for my eyes with the stiff fingers again, as quick as a cat. Her nails cut the skin below my eyebrows as I dropped my head. She was strong, for her size, and she didn't fight like the girl who had let Cornejo slap her three times without a comeback. I had all I could do to protect myself from her teeth, head, toes, knees, fingers and elbows before I got a satisfactory grip on both of her elbows from behind and could keep her at arm's length. Holding her that way, I steered her toward the door.

She let her knees buckle. I had to bring her closer to me to hold her up, and she kicked me in the shins with both heels, so hard that my eyes watered. When I pushed her away, she let her knees sag again.

This time I let her go down, still holding her elbows. I was mad. I didn't give a damn if Berrien was asleep for a hundred years, I was going to drag that fighting wildcat into his cabin if I had to sew her up in a piece of sailcloth first. I looked around for something to tie her with.

All this time we hadn't made a sound other than the hisses and grunts knocked out of us by the fight. We were both breathing hard, but not so hard that we missed the tinkle and bang of Berrien's handbell falling to the deck in the next cabin.

Ana Luz said, "The bell! *Por Dios,* let me go!"

"I'll take you there. Just stand up and start walking."

"No! No! Let me go! Something has happened! He needs me!"

She began to struggle again. I said, "I thought you told me he was drugged."

"He was! He is! Something has happened! For the love of God, let me go!"

She wasn't faking. I let her go.

I was right at her heels when she reached Berrien's cabin. The portholes were still black, and the door was closed tight. It swung open when she pushed it.

The cabin was completely dark. The porthole covers had been shut, as I found out later, so the only light entering the cabin came through the doorway. And I blocked the doorway as Ana Luz stepped inside.

If the light switch was to the right of the door, where it belonged, I couldn't find it. I said, "Where are the lights?"

"I'll get them. Wait."

Her shadow moved toward me.

At least I thought it was her shadow. I didn't have time to think much about it, because all of a sudden I got all the lights I could use in a lifetime—pinwheels, skyrockets, flares and four-alarm fire rolled into one beautiful sunburst that started at my chin, exploded behind my eyes, and burned out into a nice restful gray as I went to sleep.

4

I was lying across the sill in the doorway when I woke up. My jaw felt as if it had been blown off, but it was still where it belonged when I reached for it. So was the package taped to my ribs.

The lights were on. Berrien lay on the deck by his bunk. The mattress had been pulled out over the side of the bunk, and the sheets and blankets were in a heap on the bare springs. The rest of the cabin looked the same. Somebody had gone through it like a tornado.

Ana Luz was kneeling at Berrien's side. She had his hand in hers, and there were tears in her eyes. She didn't say anything when I got to my feet and closed the door, just knelt there holding his limp hand.

I said, "Dead?"

She nodded.

There weren't any marks on his body that I could see. His pajamas were unbuttoned, open across his chest. His face was peaceful, which didn't necessarily mean that he had died peacefully. Dead faces relax, whatever you hear to the contrary about frozen looks of terror.

I said, "Did you see who hit me?"

She shook her head, never moving her eyes from Berrien's face. Her lips moved silently.

I looked around the cabin. That was when I saw the closed ports. There was a small pile of bills and coins, a watch, and a ring on Berrien's night table. The hand bell lay on the deck where it had fallen. The box which had held the Inca jewelry on which he had paid export duties in Valparaíso was open, its customs seals broken and its contents dumped out on a chair. I recognized the gold *florero* and the piece of carved jade. If anything had been taken, other things of value had been passed up.

I said, "What killed him? How did he die?"

"I can not tell. It would not require much—a fright, a blow, anything. *Pobrecito*, he was always so close to death."

"You and I could be in trouble, if we are not careful."

She looked up quickly. She had forgotten everything but Berrien until then. I think she must have loved him, in a way, whatever kind of a double-dealing game she was playing.

I said, "I'm going to call the captain. When he, or anybody else, asks you questions, I knocked on your door a few minutes ago—your light was on because you were reading, or brushing your hair, or whatever you like—and asked you if you had seen or heard anybody go by who might have been a prowler who had searched my cabin. You said no. While we were talking, we heard the bell fall in Berrien's cabin, and ran to investigate. Tell the rest as it happened. But you never saw me before we came aboard the ship. Neither did Berrien, to your knowledge."

"Why should I lie for you? Why should I not tell the truth—that you broke into my cabin, accused me wildly of searching your things, laid your dirty hands on me…"

"One reason is that if I go to jail for smuggling, I'll do my best to take you with me, somehow. Another reason is that if the police get me, they get the package. Do you want that to happen?"

She didn't answer the question. But as I turned toward the door, she said, "Wait."

She got up off her knees, went into the bathroom, and came back with a twist of cotton and a small bottle of colorless nail polish. I had forgotten the cuts over my eyes, which would spell "roughhouse" to anybody who saw them. They couldn't be explained away as the result of a smack on the jaw, either. She wiped the blood off, then dabbed nail polish over the cuts to stop the bleeding and hide the marks. She didn't say she was sorry she had tried to put my eyes out.

The captain was on the bridge, making a last check before he turned in. He swore a green streak when I told him what had happened. He came back to Berrien's cabin, looked at the body, scratched his head, and called one of the engineers up from below to drill holes in the cabin door and its frame for a padlock. Afterward he had Sparks send a message off to the Callao police.

It was about three o'clock before he got around to me. I told him my story, starting with Harris and the prowler, and then, because his Spanish wasn't too good, offered to translate for him if he wanted to question the nurse. He told us to save it for the cops, and to get some sleep in the meantime.

I didn't sleep. I sat in a steamer chair, smoking and thinking, until the sun came over the high ridge of the Andes. An hour later we dropped anchor in Callao harbor. The police came to meet us in a launch.

The man in charge of the investigation was a little mousy fellow who wore shiny military boots and was tired of the whole business before he started. I felt better about my chances of getting off the *Talca* without trouble as soon as I saw him. He herded all the passengers into the messroom to give their stories, starting with Ana Luz.

She said her name was Ana Luz Benavides and that she was unmarried and a Peruvian citizen. She had worked for about a year as nurse and companion to the dead man. That night, she had read to him until nearly twelve, then given him his usual sleeping medicine. After he went to sleep, she had gone to her own cabin. She was brushing her hair when I knocked to ask about a prowler. We had heard the bell fall in Berrien's cabin and gone there together. Someone in the cabin had knocked me out and escaped before she turned on the lights. Berrien had been dead when she found him.

Mousy asked me about the prowler. I pushed him off on Harris, who told him just what he had told me. Mousy concluded that my prowler and the man in

Berrien's cabin had been the same person, probably a sneak thief who had knocked the bell over in his hurry, until the captain pointed out that the money and jewelry lying around loose in Berrien's cabin hadn't been touched. Mousy wanted to know if Ana Luz had any idea what the thief had been hunting for in Berrien's cabin.

She looked him in the eye and said she had no idea at all.

The police doctor said that Berrien had died of heartstrain, as far as he could tell without an autopsy, and asked what kind of sleeping medicine he had taken. Ana Luz gave him the box of pills.

"How many of these did he take?" the doctor said.

"One, ordinarily. Last night, two."

"Why?"

"He was nervous and upset. I thought it would be best for him to go quickly to sleep."

"Did the possibility that he might not awaken from a double dose of this drug never occur to you?" The doctor shook the box of pills at her. "Are you not aware that heart patients must be particularly careful with sleeping medicines? What kind of a nurse are you?"

Ana Luz flushed, but she answered steadily enough. She was not a registered nurse, more of a practical nurse and companion. The pills had been prescribed by a doctor in Lima. She had followed the instructions for their use which were on the box, if the police doctor cared to read them.

He didn't like the way she said it, but he didn't carry his questioning any further.

I had my own ideas about the extra sleeping pill. It wouldn't have done for Berrien to wake up and start ringing the bell while Ana Luz was in my cabin. But Mousy didn't even bother to ask why Berrien had been nervous and upset. He just wanted to go through the formalities and get the job finished.

Ana Luz couldn't tell him much more about Berrien, only that he didn't have any family that she knew of and that he was a naturalized Peruvian. She thought he had been born in Austria, although she wasn't sure. Mousy questioned the other passengers and learned that the poker game had broken up a few minutes after Harris and I left it. Jeff, who was banking, had most of the chips, and the game was shorthanded even before Raul followed me out. Jeff had played showdown for the rest of the chips on the table and won them all before Raul got back. He and Raul had said good night to Sparks on the boat deck and gone straight to their cabins. They hadn't known anything about Berrien's death until the next morning.

Mousy said to nobody in particular, "So at the time of the disturbance in Señor Berrien's cabin, all of the passengers, with the exception of Señor Colby and Señorita Benavides, were alone and unwatched. Any one of them could have been the person in Señor Berrien's cabin."

The fat Peruvian who had the cabin next to Berrien's jumped in at that. He had been in bed with his wife. Mousy qualified his statement. Then he pointed out that there were forty or fifty officers and crew aboard the *Talca* who didn't have wives in their beds to alibi them. Then, by one of the neatest processes of reasoning I ever heard, he concluded that, since Berrien's body bore no marks, he had very probably died in his sleep, possibly because of an overdose of sleeping medicine administered in accordance with a proper prescription. There had been no crime of violence, and no crime of theft, because nothing seemed to have been stolen from the cabin. In fact, there had been no crime of any kind to require action by the law, unless the autopsy developed something unexpected. The passengers were free to go after they had left their names and next addresses. They were reminded that the Peruvian law required them to register at the nearest *prefectura* within twenty-four hours after their arrival in any Peruvian city.

Even the captain, who had the best reasons for wanting the business cleaned up as quickly as possible, looked startled. Ana Luz said, "But what of Señor Berrien's body? And his—property?"

"Does he have heirs?"

"None that I know of."

"Did he leave a will?"

"I cannot say."

"In the absence of a will or heirs, his property will revert to the state. His body will be given Christian burial. That is all, señores. You are free to go."

I told the cops—as well as anybody else who happened to be listening—that I could be reached at the Hotel Bolívar in Lima, and took the package off the *Talca* the way it was, still stuck to my ribs. I had no trouble getting it through customs. If they searched Ana Luz this time or gave Jeff any trouble with his silver pot, I didn't know about it. I didn't wait around to watch. I was in too much of a hurry to find out just what kind of dynamite I was carrying with me.

A streetcar took me and the dynamite up to Lima from the port. At the Bolívar, I rented a room and locked the door before I peeled off my shirt.

I didn't try to save the seals on the package. My bargain had been with Berrien, not with his heirs if he had any or the Republic of Peru if he didn't. I ripped the paper off and unfolded a wad of crackly *pergamino,* parchment, covered with faint brownish-gray writing. There were three pieces of *pergamino* in the wad, doubled once across the middle, badly cured stuff that had cracked where it was folded. It had been doubled over and compressed for so long that it cracked worse when I tried to straighten it. Inside the fold was what looked like a hank of colored yarn.

I shook it out. It was a kind of short rope, about two feet long. Attached to it here and there were twisted cords of different colors. The cords were knotted all over, at different lengths and with different spacings. Shorter knotted pieces had been attached to some of the main ones. I couldn't make anything out of a mess of knotted string, so I took the parchment over to the window to try my luck in a good light.

Part of it was in Spanish. I could pick out words here and there. They were archaic and badly spelled—x's for j's, b's and v's interchanged, z's for s's and vice versa, silent h's tacked on or left off the beginning of words, as if the writer had learned his *castellano* by ear and was putting it down the way he heard it. The pigment of the

lettering had faded badly where it hadn't flaked off alto-
gether, and about two-thirds of the readable words
weren't Spanish at all. I didn't know what they were,
maybe Igorot. Some of the Igorot looked like proper
names, Ccosco and Huetín and Zaran and Saxsahua-
mán. Ccosco, allowing for this and that, could mean
Cuzco, the old Inca capital up in the *sierra* where Julie
had gone to look at ruins. I didn't know anything else
useful even after I had studied the parchment for half
an hour, except that it was old and that the message, if it
was a message, started in the middle of a sentence on
the first page and ran out in the middle of another sentence on the last page.

Berrien hadn't lied when he told me that it was an
antique. Before I did anything else, I had to find out
what else there was about it that interested so many
people. I took a taxi to the National Museum of
Archaeology, a cement copy of an Inca palace near the
Plaza Dos de Mayo, and asked to see the curator.

He wasn't in. An assistant took time out from
undressing mummies to talk to me. He looked like a
mummy himself—old, wrinkled and friendly. He had
worked with the Carnegie Institute in the States, years
before, and spoke English.

I showed him the hank of knotted cords.

"Would you mind telling me what that is?" I said.

"A *quipu*. A very beautiful one." He ran it through
his hands. "Where did you get it?"

"A friend gave it to me. What is a *quipu*?"

"An Inca message-cord. The Incas had no written
alphabet, so they used these arrangements of knots and

colors to transmit ideas and record statistics. We have a number of them here in the museum, but I don't think I have ever seen such an elaborate one." He spread the cords apart and peered at the knots. "Very interesting. *Very* interesting. Where did your friend get it?"

"He didn't say. Does it have any value?"

"Archaeologically, it is very interesting. If…"

"I mean in terms of money."

"I was going to say that if you wish to sell it, you could probably get a thousand *soles* for it from a private collector. The museum, which already has an excellent exhibit, would pay less."

A thousand *soles* was seventy dollars, more or less. I said, "I'm not anxious to sell. I'd like to know what it says."

He shook his head.

"Nobody living can tell you what it says. The art died four hundred years ago. You see, the *quipus* do not really contain connected messages, like a letter. They are more properly mnemonics, memory aids, to help a messenger or a recorder remember something which has been told him orally. All we know is that they could be used to convey a number of concrete ideas and a few simple abstractions. This white cord, for example, could mean either 'silver' or 'peace.' This yellow cord might stand for 'gold,' 'sun,' or 'royalty'—because the Inca was the son of the sun and gold was the sun's teardrops. The red one could mean 'war' or 'blood.' The knots were to jog the reader's memory in regard to what he had to say about silver, peace, gold, sun, Inca, war or blood, as the case might be."

"There isn't anyone who could tell me more about it?"

"No one. Not since the last Inca died."

He ran his fingers along the cords, studying them.

I thought about the three sheets of *pergamino* in my pocket, wondering if I ought to let him see them. If the *quipu* was worth no more than seventy dollars to a man who knew as much about it as he did, the real value of Berrien's package must lie in the *pergamino*. But they had to be connected, some way.

I said, "What language did the Incas speak?"

"Quechua."

"But they had no way of writing it?"

"No."

"Could a man who wrote Spanish write Quechua?"

"He could write the sounds he heard, phonetically. We have several old documents here in the museum, dating from the time of the Conquest, which are written in a mixture of Spanish and Quechua."

"Can I see one of them?"

"Certainly."

He brought out a couple of tattered scraps of *pergamino,* in worse shape even than mine. They had been bound between sheets of glass to preserve them. I don't know what they were, because I didn't bother to struggle with the spelling and faded print. One look was enough. They were written in the same garbled jumble of bad Spanish and Igorot that I had been poring over in my hotel room.

I said, "Can you read this?"

"No. My specialty is textiles. Ancient Quechua requires a great deal of study. There is no way to learn

64

the language as it was spoken at the time of the Conquest except through the study of documents written by Spaniards or christianized Indians of that period, who were frequently only semi-literate. Since the Quechuas themselves had no alphabet, there is no such thing as a proper spelling guide or a grammar. And many of the old words have been dropped from the vocabulary which the Indians use today."

"Were the Quechuas Incas, or the Incas Quechuas, or what? I'm pretty green on Peruvian history."

"The Incas were of Quechua stock, yes. 'Inca' means simply 'king' or 'ruler.' The Incas were a small group of ruling Quechuas who dominated the West Coast of the continent from about the twelfth century until the Conquest. If you would like to know more about them, I recommend *The Conquest of Peru* by your own countryman, William Prescott. It is one of the best books in print on the subject."

"I'll get it. Right now I'd like to know the name of somebody who can read Quechua."

"You have a document of some kind?"

"Yes."

"Where did you get it?"

"From the same friend."

He was silent for a moment. Then he said hopefully, "May I see it?"

"I don't have it with me."

"I'd be only too glad to accompany you…"

"I'm sorry. I'm not a free agent, and until I find out more about the document I'll have to keep it to myself. Maybe later I'll donate it to the museum."

He sighed with frustrated curiosity as he picked up a pen.

"There is only one man in Lima who can do a proper translation. I'll give you a note to him."

He wrote the note, folded it, and put it in an envelope. On the face of the envelope he scratched "Señor don Alfredo Berrien" and began to write an address. I stopped him.

"Alfredo Berrien is dead."

He looked up.

"What?"

"Alfredo Berrien died last night aboard a ship that brought him back from Chile. I was aboard."

"So." He put the pen down. "His heart?"

"Yes. Did you know him well?"

"Mainly by reputation. He was a collector."

The old boy got up and began to walk nervously around the room. Something was eating him, more than just curiosity now. He prowled around for a while, looked out of the window, twiddled his fingers behind his back, walked some more, and came to a sudden stop in front of my chair.

"Tell me one thing. Is this document something in which Alfredo Berrien was interested?"

"He may have been."

"Is it Peruvian?"

"I won't know until it's translated."

"If it is Peruvian, and old, I strongly advise you to turn it over to the museum, Mr. Colby. The government lays first claim to all native antiques, but they will pay you a fair discovery value. Otherwise, if you attempt to—exploit it in any way, they can confiscate it."

"I'm not planning to exploit it just now. I want to know what it says. There isn't anybody else in Lima who reads Quechua?"

"No one I would recommend. If you will leave the document with me…"

"Is there anyone else in Peru who can do it?"

He said reluctantly, "There is a man named Ubaldo Naharro in Arequipa, a collector of antiques, who has translated old writings. I will be glad to send the document…"

"Thanks. I'll take it to him personally."

The old man wasn't quite biting his nails when I left, but almost. He wanted to get his hands on that manuscript more than he wanted to live through the day. Alfredo Berrien's name certainly seemed to mean something in the old-string-and-paper business.

5

I caught up on my lost sleep during the rest of the morning. The telephone rang while I was getting dressed. When I answered it, a woman's voice said, "Señor Colby?"

"*Hablando.*"

"This is Ana Luz Benavides. May I speak to you for a moment?"

I wasn't surprised. I said, "Where are you?"

"In the hotel lobby."

"I'll be down in five minutes."

"Thank you."

She was sitting in one of the big leather chairs when I got there, her ankles together and her skirt covering her knees. She wore a dark tailored suit and a hat with a feather in it. I don't think I realized what a lady really looked like until that minute. If it hadn't been for the two little cuts under my eyebrows, I wouldn't have believed that she could hurt a fly. Or double-cross one.

We went into the *salón* and had coffee. When the waiter left us, she said, "The package is safe?"

"Which package?"

"Please, do not play with me. I have come to pay you what don Alfredo promised you. If you will give me the package…"

She let it hang.

"Why should I give it to you?"

"Because I am his daughter."

I blinked. She looked at me expectantly.

I said, "Do you expect me to believe that?"

"It is the truth."

"Show me something that says so in writing."

"I have nothing. I was brought up by people I thought to be my parents until don Alfredo told me of our relationship and asked me to be his companion. He was old and lonely and afraid of death, or he would not have told me even then."

"Why?"

"Because I am illegitimate. My mother committed suicide after I was born. He did not want me to know."

"You did not tell the police this."

"It would have served no purpose except to blacken his name and mine. I want nothing of his except the package to which I am entitled. Give it to me."

"You know what is in the package?"

"Certainly. He did not conceal anything from me."

"He tried to make it appear so."

"That was so I would not be involved if he got into difficulties." She made an impatient gesture. "Please do not keep me here explaining things which are not your affair. You were hired to bring the package here and deliver it. I am his only heir. The package is mine."

I said, "Well…" and then, "Well…" weakening. "Have you the two thousand dollars?"

She bit.

"Not in dollars. But I will give you a check for thirty thousand *soles* and go with you to the bank to cash it, if you wish."

I smiled at her.

"The payment was to be made in dollars, señorita, not *soles*. And the amount agreed upon was one thousand dollars, not two. If you did not know that, your employer told you nothing. Your whole story is a lie."

I thought she was going to try the stiff fingers on me again. I got ready to catch her wrist. She glared at me for ten seconds.

"Very well. It is a lie. How much do you want for the package?"

"It is not mine. It belongs to Berrien's heirs."

"He has none."

"Then it belongs to the state."

"The state! You *gringo* fool!"

She bit her lip.

"I'm sorry. I am upset. I must have the package, Señor Colby. It is more important to me than I can say. Is there no way I can persuade you to give it to me—sell it to me?"

She had changed, in an instant, from a cat to a soft little kitten. We were sitting side by side on a bench behind the coffee table. She put her hand on my arm and tilted her head back so that her eyelashes came down over her eyes. They were nice eyelashes, long and sweeping. Her lips barely moved as she said, "Please."

"You are wasting your time if you expect me to change my mind only because you say 'please' so nicely. I have already said no to thirty thousand *soles*. If you have any real right to the package, tell me."

She smiled quickly. It was the first time I had ever seen her smile, and it lit up her whole face. She took her hand from my arm.

"One uses whatever weapons are available," she said. "Even the truth, in the end. I need the package to buy my freedom."

"From what?"

"Slavery."

She used the word *'esclavitud.'* It had only one meaning for me. But she shook her head at my expression.

"Not as you think. Here in Peru, if you do not know our country, there are many poor people, so poor that they have neither shoes for their feet nor roofs for their heads—nor food with which to feed their families. Children starve and die, unless their parents can find another home for them. My mother was a *chola,* a woman of the *sierra.* Two of her children died because she could not feed them. She gave me, the third, as a *criatura,* to be a servant in a household where I would be fed and, with good fortune, beaten only occasionally. I had better fortune than most such *criaturas.* I was not beaten. I was fed, educated, and brought up to be what you see. In the eyes of the law, I became free when I was twenty-one. In the eyes of my *patrón,* I am still his *criatura,* as his own daughter would be, to do as he wishes. I can buy my freedom only by paying the debt I owe him. The package you have is the price."

She said it quite simply, without emotion. I had heard of the still legal institution of *criaturismo* in Peru, and knew that there were such bond-children. But she had not yet told me anything to make me change my mind about the package.

"Does it make you so unhappy, then, to have your *patrón* look on you as a daughter?"

"Have you ever owed a debt which accumulated for twenty years, señor, or known what it is like not to be your own master, not even to be able to select the person whom you will marry?"

"All daughters owe the same debt. Many marry men selected by their parents."

"They are truly daughters. It is not a debt that they can ever discharge. It comes with their blood. But I am only a *criatura,* a property of my *patrón.* Can you not understand my feeling? With the—what you have, I can become my own mistress for the first time in my life. I beg you to give it to me."

"Why do you not simply leave your *patrón?* You say you are legally free."

"It is not a legal debt that I have to pay. Please, let me have the package. I will give you anything you ask in exchange."

It was hard to refuse her—not because of her argument, which didn't impress me, but because she was a woman pleading for something important to her. And she was on the level with me, for the first time since I had known her. I was sure of that. No actress living could have faked the feeling in her voice.

I said, "If Berrien was your *patrón,* it seems to me…"

"He was not my *patrón.*"

"Is it Raul?"

"No."

"Who is it?"

"I cannot tell you."

"Does he have any right to the package?"

"As much right as anyone."

"But no more?"

She hesitated. I said, "Don't lie to me now."

"As much right as don Alfredo had, or you have."

"What is the package?"

"I cannot tell you that."

"Don't you know?"

"Yes."

"Yet you want me to turn it over to you without even knowing what it is, or who has the real right to it, or anything about it."

"I beg you to."

"Tell me what it is."

"I cannot! I cannot!" There were tears in her eyes. "Don't you think I would if I could? It's impossible!"

"Then it's impossible for me to give it to you until I know what it is. I'm sorry."

The light went out of her face. She stood up, picked up her bag, and walked away without another word.

The Faucett Airline had a ticket office there in the hotel. A flight left for Arequipa the next morning. I bought a ticket and wired for a reservation at the Hotel de Turismo. Then, because I didn't feel like sitting around thinking of dead men and the tears in Ana Luz's eyes, I bought a copy of Prescott's book in a library on La Colmena and took it to the *vermouth,* the late afternoon movie, at the Metro. After the *vermouth,* I had a good dinner and went back to the hotel ready to read about Incas, *quipus,* Quechuas and *conquistadores* and see if I could get a clue of some kind to the mysterious manuscript.

The room smelled smoky when I opened my door. I walked in, like a fool, and closed the door behind me. When I turned on the light, Jeff was sitting on the bed pointing a short-barrelled belly-gun at me.

"You sure took your time getting here," he said.

He had his feet on one of my shirts. The room was mussed up just the way Berrien's cabin had been, except that Jeff had put the mattress back on the bed so he could sit on it.

I said, "How did you get in?"

"It's a trade secret. Where is it?"

"Where is what?"

"The package."

"What package?"

"Don't stall me. I know you have it."

"What makes you think so?"

"Berrien didn't have it. I thought he had slipped it to the nurse, at first, but after I tailed her here from the ship and saw her talking to you, I knew that you were the sleeper."

"I didn't see you around when we were talking."

"You weren't supposed to. Let's have it."

He snapped the fingers of his free hand.

I said, "Did you kill Berrien?"

"That's a dumb question. Why pick on me?"

"You were the guy in his cabin."

"Is that so?"

"Nobody else on the ship could have socked me that hard."

"All right, I was in his cabin. He was dead when I found him."

"He was alive when you found him. You pointed that gun at him and he died of fright."

"It's all the same to me if you buy it or don't buy it. I'm just telling you he was dead." He snapped his fingers again. "Now unload—and be careful with your hands."

He made a lifting motion with the muzzle of the belly-gun.

I reached for the package in my inside coat pocket, using only my finger tips, and tossed it to him. He looked at the broken seals before he put it in his own pocket.

"Make anything out of it?"

"Not yet. I was hoping to find somebody who could."

"You don't have to worry now. It's in the right hands."

He stood up, motioning me over toward the bed with the gun muzzle.

"I ought to put you to sleep good and proper, but I'm too soft-hearted to slug you," he said. "I'm just going to tie you up for a while. Don't get any ideas about putting up a struggle, though, or I might change my mind."

"Soft-hearted John," I said. "How did you figure on getting it off the ship if you had found it in Berrien's cabin?"

"Swim ashore when we rounded La Punta. What do you care, anyway? You ask too many questions. Lie down."

I lay down on the bare mattress. Jeff used four of my best neckties to spraddle me out with my wrists and ankles tied to the bed frame. I could have broken his neck with a kick after he finished tying my hands and started to work on my feet, but I was a soft-hearted John myself and didn't want to hurt him. I wished I had when he finished the job and sneered at me.

"Like taking candy from a baby. You didn't even muss my hair."

"What's the percentage?" I nodded my head, which was all I could move, at his gun. "You're holding the cards."

"You're damn right I am." He patted his pocket. "I know how to play them, too. Now open your mouth, like a good boy."

He fed me a necktie, and tied a second one around my head to keep me from spitting the first one out.

When he was finished, he shoved the gun down inside his belt and waved good-bye from the door.

"So long, junior. You can work out of it if you try hard. See you around."

I worked out of it in fifteen minutes. It cost me a little skin off my wrists. I was picking at the hard knots on my ankles when somebody knocked.

"In a minute," I shouted. "I'm tied up."

He didn't wait. He pushed the door open, stepped in, kicked the door shut with his heel, and pointed another gun at me. It was my other pal from the *Talca*, Raul.

"Give it to me!" he said. "Quickly."

He was nervous. I didn't like the way he handled the gun. His knuckles were too tight. I said, "I haven't got it. Jefferson beat you to it."

"Don't lie!"

"Look around the room. I didn't tie myself to the bed like this just to keep from walking in my sleep."

I was still working on the knotted neckties. He looked around the room, saw my clothes lying on the floor where Jeff had tossed them, and realized that he was too late. The gun drooped. It lifted again when I got my ankles free and stood up.

"Put it away," I said. "If you can find Jeff, use it on him."

"That *cojudo!* How long ago was he here?"

"Quarter of an hour. Now beat it, will you? I'm washed up with the whole business."

His eyes glittered. He shifted the gun to his left hand.

"Not quite. I haven't forgotten that you hit me,

76

Colby." He took a step forward. "I owe you something for that."

"Get any ideas about paying me back, and you'll either have to pull the trigger or I'll take your pea-shooter away from you and feed it to you butt-first."

He stopped. He wanted to hit me, but not enough to take the chance that I would argue about it. I wasn't just being reckless. I knew he wouldn't pull the trigger—not there in the hotel. He finally made a half-hearted search of the room, still holding the gun on me, kicking my clothes around with his foot and messing them up even worse than Jeff had left them.

I said, "How's your illegitimate distant cousin this evening?"

His lips tightened. I said, "Tell her that Jeff was the man in Berrien's cabin. He says that Berrien was dead when he got there, so that extra sleeping pill may not have been such a good idea after all."

He pretended not to hear. I tried again.

"And tell her that any time she wants you slapped around, just let me know. I'll be glad to cooperate."

That got him. He called me five of the dirtiest names in the Spanish vocabulary as he backed out of the room and pulled the door shut between us.

I locked the door, picked up my clothes, threw them into my suitcase, made the bed, and crawled in. Reading didn't interest me any more. I went to sleep thinking of the *quipu* and the three sheets of *pergamino* safely tucked away in the big hotel safe downstairs, and hoping that Jeff would enjoy the comic book I had wrapped up in the package he had worked so hard to get.

6

Arequipa was unexplored territory to me. I knew Lima and the towns along the coast pretty well, but not the Peruvian highlands. It was early Sunday morning when the plane put me down at the airport, and the church bells were ringing. The drive into town, five or six miles from the airport through irrigated terraces of bright-green alfalfa and yellow-green stands of corn, was a concert of bells and jackasses, thousands of them, all screaming at once to welcome the sun. Nobody welcomed me, not even the Hotel de Turismo. They had my wire, but no room.

I wanted to park what I was carrying more than I wanted to park myself. I said to the clerk, "Do you have a safe?"

"A small one, señor."

"Would it be possible to leave an envelope with you for safekeeping?"

"There would be a small charge by the management."

"Clearly."

I had left the *quipu* in Lima, figuring it was just extra weight as long as no one could read it. I wrote my name across the flap of the envelope holding the three sheets of *pergamino* and gave it to the clerk, along with a ten-*sol* bill the management would never see. After I watched him put the envelope in the safe, I asked him where I ought to go to find a place to hang my hat. He recommended a *pensión* down the street.

I wasn't too happy about it when I set out for the *pensión*. South American *pensiones* are mostly scratch-houses. I expected to end up at a flea-bin like some of the others I had stayed at, full of smells and dirty kids, with chickens wandering through the *comedor*. What I found was half an acre of overgrown garden surrounded by a high wall, with a big rambling barn of a house set down in the middle of it. A crusty old dame sitting on the porch eyed me as I came up through the garden lugging my bag.

"What's your name, sonny?" she asked me, before I could say hello. Her voice had a New England twang.

"Al Colby. I'd like…"

"Had breakfast?"

"Not yet. I…"

"Better get along inside, then. Eat your meals on time or you don't eat. Leave your bag there."

"Have you got a…?"

"Twenty *soles* a day. Don't tip the servants. They're a worthless bunch of hounds, and I don't want 'em getting ideas. Run along, now."

"Thanks. Where…?"

"You want breakfast or don't you?"

Right there I gave up trying to slip a word in edgewise. She was an American, the boss of the joint, who had lived in Arequipa for sixty years. Everybody called her Abuela, grandma. She ran a clean place and kept her guests, mostly tourists, wondering how long it would be before they found their bags out in the street.

If she didn't like their table manners, she told them so. I heard from one of the guests that Julie, the blonde fluff who had left the *Talca* at Mollendo, had stopped off overnight at the *pensión* on her way up to Cuzco. Right in the middle of dinner, the old dame told her she looked like a fallen woman, and went on to lecture the other guests for a solid hour on the evils of lipstick. She didn't like interruptions, either. If you dropped a fork, she put the evil eye on you.

I never gave her any trouble. I had breakfast by myself that first morning on the *terraza,* up on the roof. There was a tremendous snow-capped volcanic cone rearing up behind the town, probably five or ten miles away but looking so close in the thin mountain air that it practically kept me company while I ate. It was all the company I wanted. The *prefectura* wouldn't be open on Sunday, so I didn't have to check in right away, and I probably couldn't find Naharro until Monday if I tried. All I had to do for the rest of the day was lie around in the garden, eat, sleep, and read *The Conquest of Peru*.

Up until then, about all I knew of the Conquest was that Francisco Pizarro had managed it, and that his bones rested in a glass case in the first chapel to the right as you enter the cathedral facing the Plaza de Armas in Lima. If Mr. Prescott did him justice, he was the number-one gangster of all time. With a handful of men, fewer than two hundred when they captured the ruling Inca in the middle of his own armies, he conquered the West Coast of South America from Chile to the equator, carried off loot worth tens of millions of dollars, and wiped out an entire civilization in the space of a few years, leaving a record of treachery, cruelty, double-dealing, greed, bravery and shortsightedness unequaled in the history of the world. The book was a thriller in blood and gold. I forgot that I was looking for something that might make Berrien's manuscript have meaning, and just read, comfortably sprawled in a chair under a tree in the quietest corner of the garden.

Jeff found me there, late in the afternoon.

He moved quietly. I didn't know that he had caught up with me until he said, "Hello, smart guy."

I closed the book. He said, "You want to hand it over without a fuss, or shall I take it away from you?"

I held out the book. He slapped it from my hand.

"Don't give me any more trouble! Hand it over!"

"I forget where I put it."

He looked around the garden to make sure we were alone. His face was nasty.

"O.K. I'll just bounce you a little until you remember."

I suppose that he hadn't mixed with anybody of his own class for so long that it made him careless. Or maybe he thought that because I hadn't put up a struggle the first time, I would let him rough me around this time without argument. Anyway, he came at me as wide open as a man in a barber chair.

I stood up and hit him about an inch below the breastbone. It didn't knock him out, but it paralyzed him. He went down like a plank and lay there, struggling to breathe, his face the same dirty blue Berrien's had been during his attack. While he was still helpless, I felt inside his belt, to be on the safe side. The gun wasn't there.

"Keep your hands off me after this," I said. "I'm tired of being pushed."

When his lungs began to work again, he got up and brushed his pants. I had picked up the book, but I didn't open it. I didn't know what he was going to do. Neither did he. The punch in the belly had cooled him down without curing him. We stood there, eyeing each other like a couple of gamecocks getting ready to jump and slash with the spurs. Little gray doves in the trees over our heads went BR-A-A-A-CK! at us, urging us to fight.

I said, "Before you get any new ideas, I'm not carrying it with me and you can't find it. I knew you'd follow me, sooner or later."

He grunted, making another swipe at his pants. The tension began to ease.

"How did you pick up my trail?" I said.

"They knew at the Bolívar that you had left in a Faucett jitney. I followed you to the airport and asked questions."

"Did you enjoy the comic book?"

He grinned, suddenly.

"I underrated you. I guess I've been underrating you all along. Let's make a deal."

"What kind of a deal?"

"I'll give you five thousand dollars for it."

"No."

"What will you take?"

"It isn't mine to sell."

"It isn't anybody's to sell. You just happen to have it, and I want it."

"I don't know what it's worth, then. I've got to find out what it is before I do anything with it."

"How are you going to find out?"

"I don't know." I showed him the title of the book I had been reading. "If I get a chance to finish this without any more interruptions, I may make something out of it."

He didn't take the hint. He said, "You'll never get anything out of that."

"Then I'll have to find somebody who can translate the—whatever it is I've got."

"The manuscript. Never mind the smokescreen. I know what it is."

"…the manuscript, and see what it says. There's a man here in Arequipa who can read Quechua…"

"Not Naharro? You're not going to Naharro?"

"That's what I had in mind."

He groaned.

"You damn fool, Naharro has been after it as long as I have, as long as Berrien has. Every collector in Peru has been looking for it for years. The minute you turn it over to Naharro for translation, you're through. He can tell you it's a recipe for apple strudel, if he wants to. You'll never know the difference, and he'll have it."

"He won't have anything that will do him any good, the way I'm going to give it to him."

"How are you going to give it to him?"

"It's another trade secret—like opening hotel-room doors."

"He'll piece it together, however he gets it. Don't go to Naharro, whatever you do. He's a bigger crook than Berrien ever was. Give it to me. Sell it to me. Or come in with me and I'll make you more money than you can count in a million years! We'll go partners! I tell you, if you give me two days alone with that manuscript, I'll lead you to…"

He shut up. He had almost become excited enough to spill the beans. I was holding my breath, waiting for him to go on.

I said, "What is it?"

"Why should I tell you?"

"Because I may give you a piece of it, if you play ball. I know the thing is worth money. I've got it, and unless an heir to Berrien's estate turns up, I'm going to keep it. You might be able to cut yourself in by telling me what you know."

"Half?"

"I'll tell you when I know how much half is worth."

"Millions," Jeff said hoarsely. "Ten millions, twenty millions, fifty millions, God knows how much." He saw my expression, and grabbed the book from my hand. "You think I'm talking through my hat. How far have you got with this?"

"I've covered the first two thousand murders."

"Did you get to Atahualpa's ransom?"

"Not yet."

He opened the book and went through the pages as if he were hunting for something on familiar ground.

"Atahualpa was the last Inca, except for a string of Spanish stooges and hopefuls. Pizarro captured him in

Cajamarca. To buy his freedom, Atahualpa offered to fill a room with gold as high as a man could reach. The room—here it is: 'The apartment was about seventeen feet broad by twenty-two feet long, and the line around the walls was nine feet from the floor. This space was to be filled with gold, but it was understood that the gold was not to be melted down into ingots, but to retain the original form of the articles into which it was manufactured, that the Inca might have the benefit of the space which they occupied. He further agreed to fill an adjoining room of smaller dimensions twice full with silver, in like manner, and he demanded two months to accomplish all this!' ž

Jeff flipped a couple of pages.

"The rooms were never filled. Pizarro killed Atahualpa before Atahualpa's *cargadores* finished bringing the stuff down from Cuzco, his capital. Pizarro figured he might as well take Cuzco himself and make a clean sweep. But what there was in that one room melted down, according to Prescott, to 'one million three hundred and twenty-six thousand, five hundred and thirty-nine *pesos de oro,* which, allowing for the greater value of money in the sixteenth century, would be equivalent, probably, at the present time, to near three millions and a half of pounds sterling, or somewhat less than fifteen millions and a half of dollars.' ž

Jeff slammed the book shut.

"That was written a hundred years ago." His eyes burned. "Today, it would be nearer thirty million—just the bullion alone. Nobody can say what the stuff would be worth in its original form—plate, jewelry, statues, ornaments that collectors and museums all over the world would bid for. You saw that pot I picked up in Mollendo, two dollars worth of silver with animal figures hammered into it. I sold it yesterday morning in Lima for seven thousand five hundred *soles*—and I could have got more by shopping around except that I was in a hurry to follow you. That was silver. This is gold—pounds of it, tons of it, mountains of it, nobody knows how much! Nobody can say what it's really worth! Pick a figure out of the air!"

"I still don't get it. What does the manuscript have to do with Pizarro's loot, if he got away with it? Didn't he take it out of the country?"

"He took what he could get. It was a drop in the bucket compared to what he missed! Every ounce of gold in Peru—and there were mines working all over the country—belonged to the Incas, the ruling family, because they were children of the sun and gold was the sun's tears. They had no currency and no need for it. They made statues with it, vases, ornaments, jewelry. They paved the floors of their temples with it. In Cuzco, they ran gutters of solid gold around the Temple of the Sun to carry off rainwater, and set gold plates into the stone walls just for sparkle. Silver was so common that the *conquistadores* used it to shoe their horses. When Pizarro killed Atahualpa and set out to loot Cuzco, the Inca priests knew what was coming. They hid tons of treasure, fifty times as much as they had sent down to Cajamarca for the ransom—buried it, dumped it into lakes, threw it into rivers—before they ran. The high priest, the Villac Umu, kept a record of the hiding places so that it could be recovered after the Spaniards were driven out of the country. He couldn't write, but he made a *quipu*, a message-string, to help him remember the details. When he died, he passed instructions and the *quipu* on to his successor. There was nobody to follow the second high priest. The line died with him. But he had learned to write. He wrote the whole story on a dozen pieces of parchment, wrapped them around the *quipu*, and died holding the message in his hand because he had no one to give it to."

"How many pieces of parchment?"

"Twelve. You ought to know. You've got them."

"That's right. Go ahead."

"The message disappeared when the last high priest died. Garcilasso de la Vega, who was a nephew of Atahualpa, spent a lifetime looking for it, and wrote a history of the Conquest in which he tells the story. But nobody ever heard of the manuscript again until some fool *hacendado* in Chile wrote to the National Museum of Archaeology in Lima saying he had come across a strange parchment and an Incan *quipu* that might interest the museum, at a price. While the museum was fiddling around trying to make up its mind, Berrien got wind of it somehow. I was keeping an eye on Berrien because—for my own reasons—and when he went to Chile himself, I knew it was something big. He never traveled any more than he had to. I followed him. He paid the *hacendado* five thousand dollars American for the thing. I found that out afterward, talking to the *hacendado*. From what he told me, and from what I knew about Berrien, there was only one manuscript he would have paid that much for. I booked passage on the *Talca* so I could get it away from him. You know the rest of it."

I didn't know the rest of it. I said, "What was your grudge against Berrien, and why were you keeping an eye on him?"

"It doesn't matter now."

"It matters to me. Let's have it."

He shrugged.

"He gypped me on a deal. He was a fence. The government lays first claim to all archaeological discoveries, and Berrien made good money buying stuff, or taking it on consignment, from sharp-shooters who picked up odds and ends here and there and couldn't dispose of them any other way. I was one of the sharp-shooters. I opened a *chullpa*, a grave, up near Macchu-picchu, and found a couple of pretty good pieces of jewelry—small stuff, gold and emeralds, easy to market. Berrien took it from me on consignment. The next thing I heard, the government had confiscated it. Berrien said his foot slipped when he tried to sell it, but I found out afterward that he had made a deal to surrender my stuff if they would look the other way while he disposed of some other stuff of his own. I was going to pinch the manuscript from him at my first chance, and he knew it."

"Did you kill him?"

"I told you once, no. He was dead when I got into his cabin. Before he learned I was aboard, I found out from the nurse that she gave him sleeping pills, and I was watching his porthole all night from the messroom to see his lights go off. I was about five minutes behind you and the Englishman when you left the game. I ducked into Berrien's cabin, closed the ports, and searched the place. I knew he was dead and not sleeping when I lifted him out of his bunk to move the mattress. It made me nervous, or I wouldn't have knocked over the bell. You came rushing in with the nurse, and I clipped you. That's all."

I took a couple of minutes to chew over what he had told me. He sat and watched me, while the little gray doves went BR-A-A-A-CK! at each other in the trees over our heads and the snow-capped peaks of the *sierra* behind the town turned pink and rose from the reflection of a sunset that looked like the fires of hell burning on the horizon—or the flames with which the *conquistadores* had burned Incas alive after they stopped being useful. Prescott's blood and thunder was still on my mind.

Jeff would have made a good *conquistador* himself. He was tough, ruthless and gold-hungry. I didn't know whether or not to believe his story about Berrien, but I was pretty sure he wouldn't have let the old man's life stand in his way of getting the manuscript—or anybody's life, including my own. He was going to be troublesome if I didn't cut him in. And I needed help to find out if my three pieces of the manuscript were enough to lead to something. The only real question in my mind was whether I wanted Jeff's help or somebody else's.

I said, "Did you know that the nurse was trying to get the package away from me?"

"No." He was plainly surprised. "How did she get on

to it? Berrien was as close-mouthed as a clam about his business."

"She knew about it, all right. I think she sent a radio message to that young *peruano*, Cornejo, to meet the ship at Mollendo and give her a hand. He tried to take it from me with a gun in Lima the same night that you did."

"I wonder who he is? I know all the collectors in Peru. I never heard of anybody named Cornejo."

"He might be another sharp-shooter."

"I know most of the sharp-shooters, too. He must be a new one. But if he's trying for it, you're going to need the kind of help I can give you." Jeff held out his hand. "Make a deal with me, Colby. Give me half and I'm your man. I can translate the manuscript as well as anybody else, I know the racket inside out, and I can handle plenty of trouble. How about it?"

I looked at his outstretched hand. It had been a fist when it knocked me silly in Berrien's cabin. And I still remembered the hard knots it had tied around my wrists and ankles.

I said, "I'll think about it—carefully."

7

Besides jackasses and church bells, another sound I learned to associate with Arequipa was the gurgle of running water. The *municipalidad,* city and surrounding farms, sprawled along the bed of a river that poured down out of the *sierra* and laid a twisting green streak across the bare desert that stretches from the Andes to the sea throughout the length of Peru. Every inch of the river bed was under cultivation. The Arequipeños had tapped the river higher up with an irrigation ditch that brought the water by gravity to a point above the town, and night and day you could hear water gushing through sluices down across the *chacras,* the garden patches that fed eighty thousand people and their livestock. The irrigation ditch marked a line like a stretched string between the bare, burned desert above and the rich greenness of market gardens and alfalfa patches below.

One of the sluices fed the garden of the *pensión.* It ran under my window. The night after I talked to Jeff, I finished reading Prescott. The last few hundred murders, tortures, burnings and massacres were too much for me. I fell asleep and dreamed that I was listening to the gurgle of a stream of blood flowing through a gold trough that started in the Temple of the Sun in Cuzco and ended somewhere outside my dream. A lot of people were in the dream: Pizarro, Atahualpa, Berrien, Ana Luz, Cornejo, Jeff. There was fighting, and men in golden armor on silver-shod horses chopped at me with jeweled swords while I tried to run with half a ton of gold in my arms. I woke up dripping with sweat that I thought was my own blood, for a minute. I hadn't had a nightmare like that since I was a kid.

But it would have taken a lot more than a nightmare to stop me after I had listened to Jeff's story of the last high priest. When I had checked in at the *prefectura,* I looked up Ubaldo Naharro's address in the phone book. His house turned out to be a big place in the Vallecito district, between the *plaza* and the river. It was built of *sillar,* the solidified volcanic ash that cuts like hard cheese. The entrance was an Incan temple doorway, flat lintel and all, covered with intertwined carvings of animal figures, faces, vines, snakes and what have you. One of the snakes had a pushbutton where his eye should have been.

I pushed it. A *chola* with no front teeth let me in, asked my name, and went to call don Ubaldo.

He surprised me. From what I knew about old-line conservative *peruanos,* I expected to get at the best a stiff bow and a chilly, polite welcome, probably standing in the hall while I told him my business. Instead, he shook my hand, took me into his study to talk, and offered me one of the black stinkers *peruanos* call cigarettes. If he was the crook that Jeff had said he was, at least he had good manners.

The study was quite a place. The walls were lined with books in five languages, mostly about Incas and the Conquest. I recognized a translation of Prescott among the others. The windows were barred with heavy iron *rejas.* On top of the bookcases stood a gold *florero,* something like the one Berrien had taken out of Chile, a gold ceremonial mask, several good silver pieces, and a stone idol. A tall glass case in the corner held a mummy, all skin and bones except for gold breastplates, a hammered plate of gold over the loins, and gold jewelry at the ears, neck, wrists and ankles. A feather mantle in good condition was framed on the wall. On the desk stood a microscope, a big reading glass, and an old leather-bound book falling apart at the seams.

Naharro himself was a stocky man with the yellow skin and swollen eyelids that go along with chronic liver trouble. He was as bald as a cueball, either because he had no hair at all or shaved what little he did have. His lack of hair made it hard to judge his age. He was quite a bit older than I was. That was all I could make out of him.

He spoke *castellano* like a Spaniard. After the preliminaries, I said, "A man at the Inca museum in Lima gave me your name. He told me that you could read ancient Quechua."

"That is true."

"I have a document, partly in Quechua, that I want translated. Can I hire you to do it?"

"What is the nature of the document?"

"I'm not sure. That is why I want it translated. I think that it dates from about the time of the Conquest."

"I can translate it for you, if it is readable. I will charge you nothing. Such things are my interest."

"You will not know what it says."

He looked at me sharply. "What do you mean?"

"You will not see the entire document. You will see portions of a photograph containing the words I want translated in such order as I may give them to you."

He didn't like that. He said, "It would be impossible. Without knowing the sentence structure, nobody could make a translation."

"You could tell me if a particular word meant horse or dog or rabbit, couldn't you?"

"Probably. But…"

"That is all I want. I can connect the words myself."

"Is the document so—secret, then?"

"I have reason to believe that it contains valuable information."

"A guide to lost Inca treasure, perhaps?"

"Perhaps."

He shook his head.

"There are hundreds of such stories, señor. Every *borrachón* on the West Coast has one he will sell you for a drink and a handful of *soles*. I have investigated several of them myself. They are all fairy stories. But if you believe that there is something in the document which I may turn to my own use, I can assure you that my reputation as a…"

"I do not question your reputation, señor. It is simply that I do not want anyone but myself to know what the document says. I am willing to pay whatever fee you wish to charge for a translation on my own terms."

I thought he was going to turn me down. He fiddled with the microscope on the table, making the barrel slide up and down on its guides, frowning at nothing. Finally he said, "Do you have the material with you?"

"No. I will bring it tomorrow, if you accept my offer."

"Bring what you wish in the morning. I will see what I can do, although you make it unnecessarily difficult."

"And the fee?"

He waved his hand.

"The fee is not important. Perhaps I will charge you nothing." He looked at me under what would have been his eyebrows if he had had any. "Another of my interests is working puzzles."

I wasn't afraid that he would make anything out of the puzzle I was going to give him. I went back uptown and hunted around the plaza until I found a store in the Portal de Flores that stocked photographic supplies. The place was jammed full of electrical equipment, radios, record players, cameras, books, magazines, all the luxury imports that ninety-five percent of the population couldn't touch in a million years. There was a sign over one of the counters that guaranteed twenty-four-hour delivery on films left for development.

I asked the girl who came to wait on me if there was a dark-room attached. She thought I was making her some kind of a proposition, at first, but she finally called the manager. He said yes, there was a dark-room. He was pretty doubtful about letting me use it. We settled at twenty-five *soles* an hour, plus costs.

I went on up to the hotel, got the envelope out of the safe, and took it back to the dark-room. The house photographer volunteered to give me a hand. I didn't see any harm in it, as long as I was there to make sure he didn't get away with an extra print. We peeled off our coats and went to work.

He had a pretty good set of equipment. We photographed each sheet of parchment separately, first with a floodlight square on, then at an angle and finally from behind. When we blew the prints up to about double the original size, one set looked as good as the original. I was ready to quit.

The photographer said, "I can do better if you wish me to, señor."

"How?"

"Here, where the ink has faded. And here, where it has flaked away. With infra-red, I can bring back the scratches of the pen, if they are there."

"Is there infra-red film in Arequipa?"

"Of a surety. We stock it here in the *almacén*."

He went to get it.

It was pretty old, but we tried it. We borrowed half a dozen electric heaters from the front of the store, searchlight-shaped things with a polished metal reflector focusing the rays of a single heating element, and set up the whole battery on a table in the dark-room. It got so hot in that stuffy little cubbyhole when all six heaters were going full blast that I was afraid the film emulsions would melt. But the photographer, his shirt sticking to his back and his face streaming sweat in the dull red glow of the heaters, shot a whole pack of film at my three pieces of *pergamino* before we got out and cooled off.

When we developed his negatives, I knew I could throw my own away. The infra-red had picked up every scratch that the pen had made. It had picked up a lot of other scratches, too, as well as the crisscross of lines made by the fiber of the parchment itself, but the message was there—complete, as far as it went. There was still no beginning and no end.

We made three blow-ups of the film. I burned everything else in a wastebasket and gave the photographer fifty *soles* for his help. After I had settled up with the boss, I carried the wet prints away with me in a picture magazine lined with blotting paper. The magazine was one of those Mexican things with a bosomy woman on the cover, full of smutty jokes and pictures of girls in G-strings and black stockings. It was the right size to hold the prints, whatever anybody thought of my literary tastes.

I was so anxious to get started that I didn't bother to go back to the hotel to leave the *pergamino* in the safe. I wished I had when I ran into Jeff, prowling restlessly around the garden of the *pensión*. He couldn't have known what I was doing, but he suspected plenty.

"Where have you been?" he growled at me.

"What's it to you?"

"You've been to see Naharro, you sucker. You might as well donate the manuscript to him and go home."

"You might as well go home yourself. I've got everything under control."

His eyes narrowed. They flicked uncertainly to the magazine under my arm, then back to my face.

"I thought I was going to get a cut."

"Maybe you are. That doesn't mean I need your help."

"You think you can handle it yourself?"

"I know I can handle it myself."

I wanted to brush him off, once and for all. I didn't trust him, and he made me nervous hanging around. I didn't trust Naharro, either, but I could handle one crook better if another one wasn't sniffing at my heels all the time.

I said, "I'll make you an offer. I'll give you a piece of

whatever it is—I won't say how much, but it will be something—if you blow. Get out of Arequipa and leave me alone. Otherwise you can go lay an egg."

He gave me a hard, level stare. Abuela came out on the porch and yelled that we were late for lunch, and if we didn't want to eat according to schedule we could move up to the hotel any time we felt like it.

"I'll take my chances," Jeff said shortly.

He turned on his heel and walked away.

I didn't go in to lunch. I spent the afternoon and most of the evening locked in my room operating on one of the prints with a razor blade. It was a slow, tricky job, and took a lot of patience to cut each word clear without clipping another. A little more than two-thirds of the words were in Quechua. All of these I had to cut out and jumble up so that Naharro wouldn't be able to make anything out of them.

There were two hundred and seventeen slips of paper when I finished cutting, each with one word on it. I couldn't number the slips of paper I was going to hand him, because it would have given away the sequence, but I had to keep the sequence for myself. While I was trying to work out a scheme, I realized that I was as hungry as a wolf. It was after dinner-time, a second meal missed. I expected Jeff to be making another try at me soon, and I was too tired to think up a safe hiding place for the stuff in the *pensión*. I didn't want to walk out through the garden, either, because the trees and bushes along the path grew thickly enough to cover anybody who felt like knocking me over the head and going through my pockets. I stuffed the *pergamino* and the photographic prints, cut and uncut, between the pages of the picture-magazine, slipped it inside my shirt, put a razor and toothbrush in my pocket, and left by way of the window. At the last minute I took Prescott along for company.

There was a ten-foot drop from the window to a cobblestoned alley running along the back of the *pensión*. The alley was dark, so I didn't see the irrigation ditch until I landed in it, ankle deep. I was pretty messy when I reached the hotel, but I felt a lot safer.

They had a room open this time. Before I registered, I borrowed a fresh envelope and went to the washroom to take the magazine out of my shirt and the *pergamino* out of the magazine. I put the *pergamino* in the envelope, sealed it, wrote my name across the flap, and gave it to the clerk to put back in the safe. I still had work to do on the prints.

The clerk was twirling the dial of the safe when a hand slipped into the crook of my arm.

"Mystery man!" Julie murmured. "Am I glad to see you!"

8

She was done up like a Christmas tree—over-ripe mouth, beads of mascara thick on her eyelashes, green eyeshadow, a hat with a trailing drape that wound twice around her throat and hung down her back. The only thing missing was a man on a leash.

She said, "Oh, am I glad to see you! Twenty-four hours more in this place and I'd go crazy."

"No playmates?"

She made a contemptuous gesture that took in the hotel and all of Arequipa.

"A bunch of jerks. I never saw such a country. Do you know where I've been?"

"No."

"Macchupicchu. It was bad enough in Cuzco, but after that I spent three hours bumping over a railroad track in a gasoline baby buggy and another hour on a mule, all to see a bunch of old rocks up on a mountain— with a party of schoolteachers, too. Not a pair of pants in the crowd but the guide, and he stank. It rained coming back, too."

"Why do you go to those places?"

"Oh, you meet such interesting people, traveling around." She dug her pointed fingernails into my arm. "Like you. Buy me a drink, mystery man."

"One. I haven't had dinner, and I'm hungry."

"So am I."

We had two drinks, and then I had to take her to dinner. I couldn't get rid of her. She was facing a four-day wait in Arequipa for a seat on the Lima plane, and I was the only unattached man on hand. She babbled on about Cuzco and Macchupicchu and the passes the traveling salesman had made at her during the train ride up from Mollendo and the horrible old witch at the *pensión* who had insulted her and the passes another man had made at her in Cuzco and the passes that a cute boy would have made at her at the hotel in Cuzco if he hadn't been with that sniffy nurse, the one that had been on the ship....

I stopped eating.

"Berrien's nurse?"

"I don't know what his name was. The sick man who had the middle cabin. He wasn't there, just the nurse and this cute boy named Raul. He was awfully cute. He didn't need a nurse around, either, but she watched him like a hawk. Whatever happened to the sick man?"

"He died on the ship. What...?"

"Oh, no! I missed all the excitement. How did it happen?"

"He just died. He had a bad heart. What were the nurse and the cute boy doing in Cuzco?"

"What do *you* think?" She looked at me slyly. "She didn't wait long to get a new man, did she?"

"Look. If I tell you I know they weren't in Cuzco just for whatever you think they were there for, can you give me some idea of what they were doing? Did they explore the ruins? Did they go on to Macchupicchu? Did they just hang around the hotel, or what?"

Her eyes narrowed as her featherbrain realized that I was seriously interested. She said, "What do you care, mystery man?"

"I want to know what they were doing."

"Why?"

"It's my mystery."

"I'll bet that's what you were doing up on the roof of the ship that night—spying on the nurse." She smiled wickedly. "Peeping Tom! You should have peeked into *my* cabin. You would have seen something."

"I'll bet I would have, too. What were they doing in Cuzco?"

"You'll have to trade. Tell me why you want to know, first."

"She's my grandmother."

"I suppose that…"

She stopped. Her eyes sparkled mischievously. She clapped her hands.

"Now I've got something that you want, mystery man. Oh, you're going to have to be nice to me! Tonight we'll see what kind of excitement there is in this graveyard, and tomorrow…"

"Tonight I've got work to do."

I signaled to the *mozo* as I stood up. She wasn't going to tell me anything useful, and she was beginning to get in my hair.

She got in my hair even more when I picked up the picture-magazine holding the photographs. She grabbed it out of my hand.

"So that's the kind of work you do." She flipped it open and whistled. "Some…"

The rest of it was almost a shriek. Several people in the dining room turned around to stare. I hadn't intended to hurt her, but I must have clamped down pretty hard, because I didn't want her to turn another page and see the prints. When I took the magazine out of her hand, she bared her teeth at me, rubbing her wrist.

"I like rough men, but not too rough," she said softly. "Don't ever hurt me like that again, damn you."

We left the dining room together. She went into the

cantina without another word. I went on up to my room.

I had thought out a scheme by then. With a second print of the manuscript as a record sheet, I numbered all the Quechua words in sequence, one to two hundred and seventeen. Then I sorted out the slips that corresponded to numbers one, four, seven, ten, and so on, seventy-two in all. I numbered these on the back from one to seventy-two, but I picked them up at random, so that number one was marked 54, number four was 17, number seven was 33, the sequence mixed all around. As I numbered the slips, I wrote their markings down opposite the true numbers on my control sheet. When I got through, I had one-third of the slips ticketed as neatly as a cold deck of cards. Naharro would have a fine time making anything out of them. And I still had two-thirds of the slips to give him after he finished with the first batch, plus all the Spanish words.

After I had finished, I put the stuff back in the magazine, rolled up the carpet, and slipped the magazine under the spot where a leg of the bed rested. I put the carpet back, the bed on top of the carpet, myself on the bed, and Prescott's book on my chest for good measure, with two pillows behind my head and the reading lamp arranged just right.

This time I skipped over the bloody parts and stuck to the stories of treasure. According to Prescott, who didn't sound like a sucker for tall stories, the Incas had more gold than they knew what to do with. Even the *conquistadores* never realized how big a jackpot they had hit. Prescott quoted dozens of stories of loot hidden from the Spaniards, although he seemed to find some of the yarns hard to swallow. I didn't learn anything new about the *quipu* of the high priest, but there was one tale which Prescott borrowed from an earlier author with his own comment that "...the tradition, in this instance, he thinks well entitled to credit. The reader will judge for himself."

This was the story:

"It is a well-authenticated report, and generally received, that there is a secret hall in the fortress of Cuzco where an immense treasure is concealed, consisting of the statues of all the Incas, wrought in gold. A lady is still living, doña María de Esquivel, the wife of the last Inca, who has visited this hall, and I have heard her relate the way in which she was carried to see it.

"Don Carlos, the lady's husband, did not maintain a style of living becoming his high rank. Doña Maria sometimes reproached him, declaring she had been deceived into marrying a poor Indian under the lofty title of Lord or Inca. She said this so frequently that don Carlos one night exclaimed, 'Lady! do you wish to know whether I am rich or poor? You shall see that no lord nor king in the world has a larger treasure than I have.' Then covering her eyes with a handkerchief, he made her turn around two or three times, and, taking her by the hand, led her a short distance before he removed the bandage. On opening her eyes, what was her amazement! She had gone not more than two hundred paces and descended a short

*flight of steps, and she now found herself in a large
quadrangular hall, where, ranged on benches round
the walls, she beheld the statues of the Incas, each of
the size of a boy twelve years old, all of massive gold!
She saw also many vessels of gold and silver. 'In fact,'
she said, 'it was one of the most magnificent treasures
in the whole world!' "*

I closed the book on that. Except for the one quota-
tion, Prescott had never mentioned an Inca named don
Carlos, even as one of the stooges set on the throne by
the Spaniards after they murdered Atahualpa. And I
remembered how Naharro had sniffed at stories of lost
treasure. But I couldn't stop thinking of those statues,
each the size of a twelve-year-old boy, all of massive
gold. I found myself trying to estimate what a twelve-
year-old boy would weigh if he was made of solid gold.
There had been fourteen genuine Incas. Figuring gold
at twenty times heavier than twelve-year-old boys, and
twelve-year-old boys at a hundred pounds flat, to be
conservative, I got a ton of gold for each statue. Four -
teen tons was twenty-eight thousand pounds. Twelve
troy ounces to the pound—no, wait a minute. That's a
troy pound. Say fifteen troy ounces to a regular pound
—fifteen times twenty-eight thousand—two hundred
and eighty thousand plus one hundred and forty thousand—four hundred and twenty thousand ounces—call
it four hundred thousand—gold was about thirty-five
dollars an ounce—thirty-five times four hundred thousand—fourteen million dollars—two hundred and ten
million *soles*…

I rolled off the bed and went into the bathroom to splash cold water on my face and hands.

The bug had bitten me. I knew why Jeff's voice had been hoarse and his eyes glittering while he was telling me of Atahualpa's ransom. Up until then, I had been playing around with Berrien's manuscript because I hadn't found anyone with a good claim to it. It gave me something to do with my time, and I still had a thousand dollars to milk out of it. I stopped thinking about the thousand dollars that night, and began to dream of gold, the metal, yellow and soft and heavy, in big shining chunks. I didn't consciously think of it as my gold, or Berrien's gold, or Peru's gold. It didn't matter whose it was. I just wanted to find it, handle it, see it glitter. I had that fever that cursed Midas.

A knock snapped me out of the pipe dream. I made sure that no bulge showed under the carpet before I turned the key.

It was Julie. She smelled of whisky. Her lipstick was smeared, and her green-shadowed eyes had a glassy look. She pushed by me into the middle of the room.

"H'lo," she said sullenly.

"Hello."

"What are you doing?"

"Reading."

"Looking at pictures of girls?"

"Reading a book."

"Why don't you come down to the *cantina* and have a drink?"

"It's too late."

"I think you're just sniffy, like that sniffy nurse. You're stuck on her, aren't you?"

"No."

"You are, too. It's a waste of time. She's got a boy friend."

"That's good."

"You think you're smart, don't you?"

"No."

"Yes, you do. You think you're just the smartest guy in the whole world—just too smart and too good for anybody."

She fumbled with her purse, got it open, found a pack of cigarettes, and spilled most of them pulling one out. I held a match for her. She almost burned her false eyelashes off getting a light.

"You think I'm a tramp, don't you?"

"No."

"You do, too. Everybody thinks I'm a tramp, just because I like to have fun. Everybody else has a family or a father or a mother or a brother or somebody that wouldn't let horrible old women tell them that they wear too much lipstick." She was beginning to cry. "I haven't got anybody. Nobody cares if I'm a t-tramp or how much lipstick I wear or anything. N-nobody cares. Nobody even wants to buy me a drink in the *c-cantina*."

"I'll buy you a drink tomorrow. You've had too many for tonight. Go to bed and sleep it off."

"I don't want to go to b-bed." She wiped her eyes, smearing the mascara. "I'm lonely. I want somebody to talk to."

She sat down with a bump, nearly missing the chair.

I said, "You can't stay here."

"Why can't I?"

"Because I won't let you."

"Going to throw me out?"

She smiled, a slow, drunken, smeary smile.

I couldn't stand her around much longer. I took the smoldering cigarette away from her and put it out.

"Let's go to your room. Where is it?"

"What do we want to go to my room for?"

"Never mind. Where is it?"

The smeary smile came back; sly, understanding, expectant. She said, "Down the hall."

I took her by the arm.

We didn't meet anyone in the hall, luckily. Once she stumbled and fell into me, knocking the draped hat sideways. I put my arm around her and half carried her to the door. She had the key in her purse. I got it out, unlocked the door, and pushed her inside.

Before I could find the light, she put her arms around me. I held her with one arm, afraid that she would fall, and reached for the light switch with the other. When the lights came on, her eyes were closed. Her head hung back on her shoulders, so that I could see where a line of sun-tan makeup ended on her throat. She mumbled something.

"What?"

"Kiss me, mys'ry man."

"Open your eyes."

They opened. I took her by the shoulders and turned her around so that she was facing the mirror of the *peinador*.

It was a big mirror, nearly full length, and it gave her a good view—smeared lipstick, smeared mascara, cock-eyed hat, loose mouth, glassy eyes, rumpled clothes, everything. She rocked there for seconds, looking stupidly at herself.

"Who wants to kiss that?" I said.

Her eyes changed. She put her hands over her face and turned blindly away. The bed caught her below the knees. She fell forward on it, still with her hands covering her face.

I lifted her legs up on the bed, took off her shoes, and ran my hands over her to see if she was wearing anything that would stop circulation. She wasn't. I put a blanket over her and opened a window.

She was looking at me when I stopped at the door. I could see only one eye. It wasn't fogged, or stupid, or drunken. It was as unblinking and full of hate as a pointed gun barrel.

I switched off the light and closed the door, sure that she would have forgotten all about it by morning.

9

Early the next day, I took my seventy-two numbered slips of paper to Naharro. The toothless *chola* showed me into his study, where he was waiting for me. I spread the slips out on his desk.

"You can list the translations by number," I told him. "If there are any duplications, make a cross reference."

He looked at what I had brought him, his swollen eyelids drooping, and stirred the slips around with his finger.

"Is this all?"

"No. I'll bring you others when you have finished with these."

"I suppose the numbering has been arranged?"

"Yes."

"You do not trust me."

I didn't argue with him. He stirred the slips again, picked one up, and studied it.

"Come back tomorrow morning. I will have the translations for you then."

"Can't you do it sooner than that?"

"Whatever it is that your document concerns, señor, you say it dates from the Conquest. After four hundred years, another day or two cannot matter much."

"I am anxious to know what it says."

"This evening, then. I cannot promise anything earlier."

"This evening."

I left him still playing with the slips of paper. His liverish face was sullen.

It was all the same to me how he felt, as long as he did the job. I felt pretty good about everything. It was a bright, clear morning. Later in the day the *nevada,* the gloomy overcast of the *sierra's* short rainy season, would come down from the mountain peaks and hang over Arequipa like a moldy blanket, but at that hour there wasn't a cloud in the sky, literally or figuratively. In another couple of days I would have the translation of the manuscript and be on my way to wherever it took me. Jeff could be sidetracked when the time came for it, or even sucked along as a decoy for Ana Luz and Raul, who apparently knew enough about the story of the hidden gold to realize that the search for it would have to start in Cuzco. But that was all they knew, and I was pretty sure I could handle them, in Cuzco or any-where else. Anybody smart enough to manage a crafty old codger like Ubaldo Naharro shouldn't have any trouble with those two.

I was so busy patting myself on the back that I didn't see Jeff until I was level with him. He was leaning against a tree, half a block from Naharro's house. He fell into step with me.

I said, "You never give up, do you?"

"No."

"Have any trouble tailing me this time?"

"I knew you were doing business with Naharro. When I found out that you had skipped, I came here and waited until you showed up."

"When did you find out that I had skipped?"

"Early this morning. I searched your room."

I had to laugh. He said it as if he were telling me that he had come around to borrow a match.

"Figure on trying to search me next?"

"I'll get to that when I think it will do some good. I came to tell you that Raul Cornejo is in town."

"Why tell me?"

"Didn't you say that he tried to take it from you in Lima?"

"I told him you got it. Maybe he's looking for you."

"I hope he is." Jeff grinned, an ugly grin. "I'd like a little trouble. I'm ripe for it. But you'd better be careful."

"What do you expect to get for the tip—a kiss?"

"The hell with you!" His face flushed. "I don't care if you rot! I just don't want anybody to get that manuscript from you before I do. I don't know how Cornejo got into this, but if he tried once he'll try again."

"Is Berrien's nurse with him?"

"I didn't see her. I only saw him for a minute. He tried to get in at the *pensión* this morning, but the old *bruja* was booked up a week in advance. He went on to the hotel."

"Did he see you?"

"Nobody sees me when I don't want to be seen."

We walked back to the *pensión* together.

Jeff knew a shortcut, a twisting, cobbled *callejón* so narrow that we had to squeeze against the wall when we met a string of pack llamas laden with firewood, ugly animals that stank and spat at us as they passed. I thought Jeff had picked the *callejón* as a good place to make another play for whatever he thought I was foolish enough to be carrying with me, and I was careful not to let him get behind me. But he didn't try anything, just trudged moodily along with his thoughts. It was a strange feeling, walking with a man who wanted nothing more than to cut my throat but was going out of his way to see that nobody else did it.

Once he said abruptly, "I hope you know what you're doing with Naharro. He's a fox."

"It's white of you to worry about my business."

"I've got a piece of your business."

"You think."

"I've got a piece," he said doggedly. "Don't kid yourself that I'm not going to get it, either. You'll make it easier on yourself if you take me in. I'll get it, one way or another."

"You hope."

He didn't say any more.

At the *pensión,* I packed my clothes and told Abuela I was moving to the hotel. She grumbled about good-for-nothing guests who moved in just long enough to dirty the linen and then moved right out. I didn't tell her that her guests found it too easy to search each other's rooms for my comfort.

When I went out through the garden with my bag, Jeff watched me go. Halfway up the hill to the hotel—it was only a short walk—I looked back. He was standing at the gate of the garden, still watching me. He lifted his hand when he saw me turn around. The wave said: I'll be seeing you.

And as if having him on my back wasn't enough to keep me busy, the first person I bumped into at the hotel was Ana Luz. She was coming out the door as I went in. I wasn't surprised to see her, knowing that Cornejo was around, but I had been wondering what had brought them down from Cuzco. I hoped it was because they had learned that Jeff was in Arequipa, and still thought he had the manuscript. If that was it, helping the mistake along would be a good way to keep them all occupied.

Ana Luz didn't show any surprise at seeing me. She

looked right through me. I lifted my hat. She nodded coolly and started to pass, but I stopped her.

"Excuse me, señorita. I would like a word with you."

"I thought that we had our last words in Lima, señor."

"Perhaps a few more would be an advisable precaution on my part. Does your presence in Arequipa have any connection with my own?"

"None at all." She wasn't tall enough to look down her nose at me, but she tried.

"I am glad to hear it. I wanted to be sure you knew that the object in which you expressed an interest is no longer in my possession, and that any further approaches by you or your cousin, with or without firearms, would be a waste of time—until I recover it. I explained all this to Señor Cornejo at one time, but if he has not told you…"

"Nothing about you interests me in the least, señor. Believe me."

I bowed and stepped aside to let her pass.

I wasn't satisfied with one slap in the mouth, so I gave Julie her turn at bat as soon as I had sent my bag up to my room. She was sitting at a table in the *cantina*, alone and sober, drinking a *limonada*. She had given up the merry-widow hat and the green eye-shadow. In a print dress that brought out the points of her good figure, with her blonde hair combed and neat, she looked pretty good—even kissable. And lonely. I stopped at her table.

There was a half-empty glass in front of the chair opposite her. I said, "May I sit down?"

"No."

She didn't even lift her head. I think she smelled me. Her nostrils were distended, white at the edges.

"You look nice this morning."

"Go away."

"I'm just being friendly. If you haven't anything to do this afternoon…"

"I have plenty to do this afternoon. If I didn't, I wouldn't do anything with you."

"Don't be nasty, Julie. I'm sorry if I hurt your feelings last night."

She looked up then.

"I don't want to talk to you," she said levelly. "I don't want to have anything to do with you. If you stay here, I'm going to call the manager and tell him that you're molesting me."

Somebody came up behind me. I thought it was a *mozo,* and I was glad she spoke only English.

"I can't be that bad," I said.

"I told you not to hurt me twice." She still spoke in the same controlled, monotonous tone. "Raul, will you throw this man out, please?"

I turned around.

Cornejo was right behind me. His eyes were bright. He looked from my face to Julie's, then back at me. It wasn't lack of inclination that made him hesitate to take up her offer. I could feel him bristling, like a porcupine.

I said, "All right," and walked away.

With everybody in Arequipa damning my eyes and anxious to put a spoke in my wheel, I had to be extra careful. Raul and Ana Luz might or might not believe that I still had the manuscript, but Jeff knew. He was good at searching rooms, too. I locked my door, got the picture-magazine out from under the carpet, and numbered the remaining hundred and forty-five slips as I had numbered the first batch, making two separate sets. One set I divided into halves, laying them flat under the insoles of my shoes. The other set I dropped loose in my pocket. I wasn't over-confident about the shoes as a hiding place, but if anybody jumped me and got away with it, he should have no good reason to suspect that he wasn't getting all there was to get when he went through my pockets. And I still had two other complete prints of the manuscript, the numbered control sheet and an unmarked one.

But I couldn't leave the prints lying around, and when I took them downstairs in their girl-show cover, Raul and Julie were still in the *cantina*. Julie didn't look up as I went by. Raul did. It was like seeing a snake's head lift from its coils. I couldn't go near the hotel safe while he was watching me, so I took the prints downtown to the Banco de Credito and saw them locked away in a fire-proof vault. With that off my mind, I had nothing to do but kill time until evening.

It was the longest day I ever killed. I cashed a traveler's check at the bank, and then didn't know what to do with the money. There was no way to spend it, except for a couple of crummy movies, and I didn't feel like sitting still. I couldn't find a bowling alley, or a billiard table. Finally somebody told me there was a golf course at the edge of town.

The golf course was better than nothing, but not

much better. It was above the irrigation ditch, spread out over the desert hills, nothing but sand—fairways, greens, rough, bunkers, everything the same. Lines of white stones marked the fairways. I rented a bag of battered clubs from an old woman who had a key to the deserted clubhouse, and played eighteen holes. The *nevada* had crept down from the mountains by then, and a thick blanket of woolly gray cloud hung low over the hills, cutting the mountain peaks off at their bases. The course was empty and cold. There wasn't a blade of grass or a tree within miles. A dry, chilly wind blew across the hills, lifting sand that filled my eyes and ears. I couldn't hit a decent ball off the loose ground, or plant my feet properly, or do anything right. I was sour, the way you go sour with dice or cards, when the law of probabilities stops working for you and you can't do anything but lose. It may have been only the combination of that barren landscape, the dusty wind, the gloomy overcast, the strange gray light, but more and more the feeling grew on me that my luck had run out. Something serious was going to go wrong. Either the manuscript would turn out to say nothing, or an earthquake would wreck the bank vault, or Jeff would outfigure me somehow. I could feel trouble coming as plainly as you smell rain on a wet wind.

It was sundown when I finished three-putting the last gravelly green. I paid off the old woman who had loaned me the clubs and went back to Naharro's house.

The *chola* said that don Ubaldo had visitors, and sidetracked me into a gloomy waiting room. I waited for five minutes before he showed up.

He wasn't sullen any more. He gave me the same handshake that I had got the first time I met him, before I had crossed him up with my scheme. I asked him how he was getting along with the translation.

"Very well. I will finish what I have in a few hours."

"No difficulties?"

"More than there would have been if I could have worked from the original." He chuckled, putting his hand, liver-spotted and yellow, on my arm. "It was a clever device you invented, the cutting. I confess that I am really curious to know what the manuscript says, with its talk of precious metals and torture. I suppose there is no chance that I may see it?"

"Not until I have a full translation."

"I thought not." He chuckled again. "Perhaps it will turn out to be only another legend, and then you will sell it to me for my collection. In the meantime, I am afraid that I still need some time to finish what you have given me. Perhaps you will come back later. Or, better yet, join me in an early dinner. Afterward you can amuse yourself as you please while I finish the work."

"What of your visitors?"

He waved his hand.

"They have gone."

I accepted his invitation, because I was anxious to get the translation from him as quickly as possible. I still smelled trouble.

But I almost forgot to worry during dinner. Naharro's food was good. His liquor was good, too, and he was an interesting talker. I listened to him discuss the Conquest for half an hour, and enjoyed it, before he made a polite gesture to turn the conversation over to me.

"You are a student of Peruvian history, Señor Colby?"

"An amateur only. I find the story of the Conquest very interesting."

"It is very interesting. But the history of the empire which the *conquistadores* destroyed is even more interesting. Imagine, if you can, a truly social community—a despotism, it is true, where the Inca was a god on earth, an absolute ruler of his subjects, but a society in which no one was idle, no one went hungry, no one suffered want. Except for the Inca, who owned everything, no one was rich and therefore no one could be poor. The empire was based on a policy of peaceful conquest, negotiation, understanding, community of effort. The Incas preferred to construct roads and fine buildings, rather than wage war. They fought courageously enough if they had to, even when Spanish guns and horses proved to be too much for them, but theirs was essentially a country of peace and prosperity. Greed was unknown, because no man could lose what he had not nor strive for what could never be his. Currency did not exist. Think of that, señor. Imagine a society with no need for money, and compare it with our poor country today, backward, undeveloped, dependent on imports for its life but with no way open to earn the credit which it must have for its survival. Our whole economy is geared to your American dollars, for which we must pay fourteen, fifteen, sixteen to one—when they are available. I myself have offered sixteen to one this week without finding a single seller."

I almost laughed at the way he had worked the conversation around from the Inca empire to the subject of dollars. Everybody wants dollars in Peru, and they usually get at it in the same roundabout way, so the seller won't see how anxious they are and hold them up. But it explained his change from sullenness to cordiality, which had puzzled me, and his *soles* were as good as the next man's.

I said, "I have some traveler's checks, if you are in the market."

"Traveler's checks would be excellent. What do you ask?"

"The bank paid me fifteen this morning. You can have them at the same rate."

"That seems fair. Very fair indeed. Could you sell me—let me see—three hundred dollars?"

I countersigned three traveler's checks. He paid for them in cash, forty-five hundred *soles* in big bills that he dug out of an iron box. My traveler's checks went into the iron box, which he carried away with him to some hole of its own. When he came back, five minutes later, the dinner was over.

I read his copy of Prescott and drank coffee with *anís* while he worked on the translation. The wait brought back my jumpiness. It took him a little more than an hour to finish, mumbling over the reference books he had spread out under a lamp on the table in his study. A lot of the slips were duplications, so he had only about fifty words written down on his list when he gave it and the slips to me.

I handed him the batch I was carrying in my pocket. "Can you finish these by tomorrow night?"

"I think so. This is all?"

"There will be one more set, the last."

His heavy eyelids drooped. He chuckled.

"You are a careful man, Señor Colby. I am glad that I do not have to do business with *gringos* more often. They are too clever for me. Shall I call you a taxi, or will you walk?"

"A taxi. Your *soles* would make good bait for bandits, and the streets are dark."

I wasn't as afraid of bandits as I was of Jeff and my jinx, but Naharro didn't have to know that.

He called a taxi.

When it let me off at the hotel, I looked over the lobby and the dining room to see if I could spot Raul or Ana Luz before I went to the desk. They weren't in sight. Julie still sat in the *cantina,* just where she had been that morning, twirling the lemonade glass in her fingers. She kept her eyes on the glass as I went by.

I meant to make another try at apologizing after I had got rid of what was in my pocket. She must have been pretty miserable, sitting there alone. I said to the clerk, "Give me the envelope from the safe. I have something to add to it."

The clerk stared at me.

"But, señor! I gave it to your messenger, not half an hour ago."

It was like being hit from behind with an ax. I

couldn't move. I couldn't open my mouth, or lift a hand, or think. While I stood there, bleeding to death inside, Julie began to laugh.

10

She was still laughing when the clerk, seeing my expression, handed me a short, typewritten note. It said, in Spanish, "Please deliver to the bearer the article you keep for me in the safe," and was signed with my name. The signature looked like mine.

The clerk said, "I hope nothing is wrong, señor. I compared the signatures carefully before I surrendered the envelope."

I began to function again—not much, but enough to talk. I said, "Who brought the note?"

"A *muchacho* of the street."

Julie's laughter was getting hysterical. I walked into the *cantina* and sat down opposite her. The laughter shut off like a stream of water.

"I've been waiting for hours to see your face when you heard that it was gone." She licked her lips like an animal. "Oh, it was good! It was wonderful!"

She began to laugh again.

I let her have it out while I examined the signature of the note. From the slight unsteadiness of the pen scratches that should have been sharp and firm, and the thinness of the paper, I could see that it was a tracing. But it was smaller than my normal signature. It hadn't been taken from the hotel register. I thought back, trying to remember what else I had signed—the book at the *pensión,* a form at the Banco del Credito, a traveler's check...

Naharro!

Naharro, his liverish eyelids drooping, his bald head wagging in admiration, chuckling over the *gringo's* cleverness while I wrote my name three times for him in the cramped space left for my countersignature on the traveler's checks, and then sat around for an hour drinking his *anis* while he made use of them!

I put my hand over my eyes and tried to think, while Julie's laughter went on and on and on. She was the only one who could have known that I had something in the safe. She had seen me put it there, the first night. But she didn't know Naharro, and she didn't know what I had. There had to be an intermediary, a connection of the two points somewhere. Jeff—or Raul and Ana Luz. Jeff was the only one of the three who knew Naharro—as far as I knew. There was a lot I didn't know.

The traveler's checks, then. Naharro had known I was carrying them before he laid his trap. Either Jeff or Raul could have told him, because they had both seen me try to cash one in the poker game aboard the *Talca.* But Jeff was a lone wolf, and it had been Raul who was buying Julie's *limonadas* that morning.

I said, "You told Raul."

She nodded. Her eyes sparkled. She was cold sober, and so pleased with her nastiness that she was bubbling to tell me everything, to twist the knife for all it was worth.

"He asked me why I hated you. He told me how you had hit him. He hates you, too, and his cousin hates you. Everyone hates you." The words came out in an eager rush. "They wanted to get something you had stolen from them. He wouldn't say what it was, but it was small, and I told him about seeing you put something in the safe with your name on it. He said he knew how to get it, then, and kissed me, a nice kiss, the one you didn't want, and after he left I sat here waiting for you to come in so I could see your face. It paid for everything! It made me happy, happy, happy…"

She choked, jumped to her feet, and ran.

I went back to the desk.

The clerk eyed me curiously. I was trying to keep my face from giving me away, but my mouth felt tight and dead when I spoke to him.

"Is Señor Cornejo still in the hotel?"

"No, señor. He checked out earlier this evening."

"And Señorita Benavides?"

"She left at the same time."

It was all I needed to hear.

When I reached Naharro's house, the lights were on in a room I recognized as his study from the heavy *rejas* over the windows. I rang the bell.

Ana Luz opened the door.

I pushed by her without a word. She didn't try to stop me, or raise a fuss when I walked down the hall to the study. Naharro sat at his desk, the lamplight shining on his bald head, bending over the slips of paper I had left with him. He looked up with a frown that changed to a broad smile.

"Señor Colby! What a pleasant surprise!"

"Where is the manuscript?"

"Ah, yes. The manuscript." He pushed his chair away from the table, stretching. "You think I have it, and you want it back. You can prove a good title to it, no doubt?"

"I can prove enough title to it to charge you with forgery and theft tomorrow morning. Somewhere in this house there is a typewriter that matches the typing on the note with my signature forged to it. I take either the typewriter or the manuscript with me when I go."

"That is a stupid thing to say, for several reasons." Naharro held up a yellow hand and counted on his fingers. "The typewriter is not in the house. You have no title to the manuscript. You smuggled it out of one country and into another, twice breaking the law. You are a foreigner in a city where I have influence. And finally, you have forced your way into my house without invitation and threatened to carry my property away with you, like a common thief." He nodded at something behind me. "My son could shoot you now with impunity."

I turned around.

Raul was holding a gun on me from the doorway. It was the same gun he had used in the hotel in Lima, and his knuckles looked the same, cramped and tight. His mouth was set hard. Ana Luz stood behind him.

Naharro's voice at my back said, "There are several other things you should know, Señor Colby. You would never have had a chance to use the manuscript. To do archaeological research in Peru, you must first have a permit from the National Institute of Archaeology. I am a member of the Institute, and I would have seen to it that you never received such a permit. Had you found anything in spite of that, you would never have been able to take it out of the country, or dispose of it here. Your whole attempt was hopeless from the start. I advise you to leave Peru quietly and go back where you came from."

I was tired of looking at Raul's knuckles. I turned back to face Naharro.

"They are convincing arguments, don Ubaldo—particularly the gun. Was it by your orders that Alfredo Berrien died? Did he also break into your home and threaten to steal your property?"

"Alfredo Berrien died because his time had come to die. I had nothing to do with it."

"Perhaps your *criatura* had something to do with it. Perhaps the police would like to know how it happened that she was the nurse who gave him his last sleeping pill."

"The police have already satisfied themselves about his death. If you have any thought of going to them, I urge you not to, for your own sake. And now I have said all I intend to say to you. Will you leave quietly?"

"I have more cuttings in my pocket. Why don't you steal those, as well? They are easier to read than the original."

Raul moved, behind me. But Naharro was too smart.

He said, "They are not important, Raul. I have enough of them to make the others worthless. He hopes that you will come within his reach, which might be unwise. Stay well behind him when you show him to the door."

"Don't worry about me," Raul said. "*¡Adelante!*"

I didn't budge. He said unemotionally, in English. "I'd like to kill you, Colby. He doesn't want it that way, or I'd shoot now and enjoy it. But don't think he'll stop me if you're troublesome. Move!"

I moved.

He backed away from the doorway to let me by, and followed me at a safe distance. Ana Luz went ahead to open the street door.

As I passed her, going out, I said, "I hope you get credit for this. I can see why you wanted your freedom. Is *guagua* here the one you were supposed to marry?"

Guagua means "baby," a child in arms, too small to do anything but yell and suck and wet his pants. It wasn't much of an insult, but it was the best one I could think of. I would have given everything I owned to get Raul within reach, just then. I wanted to feel his bones crack in my hands.

Ana Luz said levelly, "I am sorry that we are enemies. It is not my…"

"Shut up!" Raul's voice was choked. "Get out, Colby!"

The door slammed behind me.

I set out for the *pensión,* walking fast.

I wasn't licked yet, but the time had passed when I could handle the job alone. I had to get a translation of one of my remaining prints in a hurry, and Jeff was the only man I knew of who could do it. Whether I liked it or not, I would have to cut him in.

He cut himself in. He was waiting for me near the tree where I had bumped into him before, but on the other side of the walk, in the shadow of a high hedge. As I went by, he mousetrapped me with an arm around my throat, his hand over my face to pull my head back and his knee in the small of my back.

"I thought you'd be along, smart guy!" he snarled in my ear. "Let's see you wiggle out of this one!"

I did my best. I tried to pull him forward, hoping to reach through my legs and catch his ankle, but his knee in my back gave him too much leverage. He had me in a clamp like a vise. My ears began to roar. I took hold of his wrist with both hands, but he had locked it tight with his other hand. I was strangling, drowning in a black whirlpool of noise, my chest bursting. I pried at his fingers, got one of them loose, and was trying to find enough strength to break it when the oxygen gave out. The whirlpool took me away.

11

The night air felt good in my lungs when I opened my eyes. I was lying on grass, looking up at stars that showed through rents in the cloudy sky. The dark bulk of the hedge was still there. From its position, it seemed to me that I should be lying on the pavement where Jeff had jumped me, instead of on grass. I puzzled over it for a while, too tired to move. My throat hurt.

It was a couple of minutes before I felt like sitting up. I had been hauled through, or under, the hedge into the field on the other side. I could hear the running water of an irrigation sluice. There was nothing to see. When I stood up, I had no shoes on.

I groped around in the dark until I found them. The insoles had been torn out, and the cuttings were gone. So was everything that had been in my pockets—money, keys, passport, traveler's checks. He hadn't left me so much as a cigarette. Even the lining of my coat had been ripped loose.

The hike to the *pensión* put me back into shape, except for the sore throat. I stumbled a little, at first—my legs felt like boiled spaghetti—but pretty soon I was going along good, stepping high and breathing deeply. Where the shadows were dark and nobody could see me, I shadow-boxed to tighten my loose muscles. By the time I reached the gate of the *pensión* garden, I was all right again, except for my throat.

The gate was closed for the night. A hunchbacked *concerje,* wrapped in a gunnysack, sat motionless on the steps inside. I croaked at him through the wicket until he woke up and let me in.

"Has the big *gringo* come in?" I asked him. My voice was like a bullfrog's.

"Fifteen minutes ago."

"Which is his room?"

"The second floor, up the outside stairway. Beyond that I cannot tell you."

"It is enough."

A dim light glowed over the stairway that led to the second floor. It was a shaky thing, added on after the building had been turned into a *pensión*, and it swung under me with each step. I went up heavily and slowly. At the top, there was a short hall with four doors. One, which was open, led to a bathroom. Two of the others, badly fitted in their frames, showed no cracks of light. The third did. I pushed at it.

It swung open. I followed it in, barely catching myself from falling. Jeff, sitting at a table on which all my stuff was spread out, looked up at me, grinning his wolf grin. The belly-gun lay near his hand.

"Well, well," he said. "Junior again. Back for a rematch?"

I blinked at him. He had the cuttings spread out in front of him, and was trying to line them up into some kind of sequence. He looked so pleased with himself that I guessed he hadn't got far enough along to find out that what he had didn't mean anything.

I weaved over to the table and reached clumsily for the slips with my left hand. He didn't bother with the gun. I looked too easy for that. When he stood up to smack me, I hooked a right at his chin, as hard as I could throw it. He went headfirst over the back of his chair and hit the wall. Before he could get up, I landed on his chest and was softening him up with both hands, taking out on him not only the sore throat and spaghetti legs he had left me but all I had put up with from Naharro and his son and his *criatura*. It didn't do Jeff any good, but it helped me.

After he stopped struggling, I climbed off and recovered the things he had taken out of my pockets. The cuttings and Naharro's list I left on the table, but I took the gun. There was a pitcher of water in a basin on a nightstand near the bed. I poured it on him until he sat up and shook his head.

"How did you like the rematch?" I croaked.

He didn't say anything, just sprawled there in the puddle I had made for him, blinking groggily. I said, "That was just to make us even. Before you try to jump me again, I'm giving you your piece. Naharro foxed me out of the manuscript. I need your help."

It woke him up better than another splash from the pitcher would have done. He said, "What happened?"

"My throat hurts too much to answer questions now. I've got a photograph of the parchment in a bank vault downtown. How long will it take you to translate it?"

"A day. Two days. I can't tell until I see it. But if Naharro has the original..."

"We've got to beat him out, that's all. The photograph is clearer than the original. He's already translated part of it from those clippings you found in my pocket, but he doesn't know that I still have a complete print, and he hasn't any reason to hurry. We can head him off if we work fast."

"Can you get the print tonight?"

"I don't know. I'm going to try. There's one other thing. Berrien only had three pieces of the parchment. As far as I could tell, they were right out of the middle of the twelve. They may not be worth a damn, or they may take us somewhere. If we find anything, we split fifty-fifty—but I market the stuff."

Jeff got up and dried his face and hair with a towel before he said anything to that.

"What do you know about marketing it?"

"I know that the government will give us a reward for

discoveries—maybe not as much as we could get some- where else, but enough. I'm not going to try to smuggle it out of the country."

"Leave it to me, then. I've got connections in La Paz, in Bolivia. I've taken stuff out before, across Lake Titicaca from Puno…"

"We're not going to take it out, across Lake Titicaca or any other way. I'm telling you now. I don't want to run up against the government. If there's anything at all to find, we'll make a fair piece of change out of it and still be on the right side of the law."

He rubbed the towel over his hair, frowning. I said, "We do it that way or not at all. Make up your mind."

He shrugged.

"O.K. But you're a sucker. Why cut the government in?"

"Because I like to travel around these countries under my own name."

It hit. His lips tightened. He had had another name, once—a name that belonged to a man with better use for a sound knowledge of archaeology and the Quechua language than sharpshooting for odds and ends of Incaic jewelry to palm off on a shady fence like Alfredo Berrien. But all he said was, "O.K. You're the boss."

He put out his hand. We shook.

"Now I'm going downstairs and use the phone," I said. "Have you got anywhere with the cuttings?"

"Not yet. I was trying to sort them."

"The sequence doesn't mean anything. Naharro's translations of the batch you found in my pocket are on that sheet of paper. The slips that were in my shoes haven't been translated yet. Go to work on them while I see if I can wake up the bank."

It took me four phone calls to get hold of the bank manager at his home. He had already gone to bed and didn't like being waked up by a bullfrog croaking at him over the telephone. The vault had a time lock, anyway.

Jeff was scowling at Naharro's list of translations when I got back to his room, comparing it with the slips that had been translated. He shook his head as I came in.

"Naharro foxed you in more ways than one. These are all sour. Nobody living can tell you what most of these words are without seeing the context. He's put this one down as *campo*, open field, but it can mean a closed *patio*, or even a closed room. And this one means 'south,' nothing but 'south.' He's put it down as 'west.' "

"He was stringing me along until he could get hold of the parchment himself. He knew what I had even before I showed up in Arequipa. Cornejo is his son."

"How did you find that out?"

"By busting into Naharro's house to get the manuscript back from him, and having Cornejo run me out with a gun just before you jumped me."

"Uh, huh. That's why I never heard his name. I knew Naharro had a son, but he sent him to college in the States and I never ran into him. Who is the phony nurse—a daughter?"

"A *criatura*. Her mother gave her to Naharro when she was a kid."

"I wouldn't mind having a *criatura* like that myself." Jeff grinned admiringly. "I suppose Naharro planted her on Berrien so she could tip him off whenever Berrien got onto something good. He must have been stealing stuff right out from under Berrien's nose. I told you he was a fox."

"Or a snake. That's a dirty way to do business."

"The whole racket is dirty business. It's the only way you can play it. The minute you sink a spade into a burial mound without a permit from the government, you're outside the law. From then on, it's cutthroat."

"Why not get a permit, then?"

Jeff laughed.

"You don't know Peru. No, we'll pay a little fine when the time comes—after we get the stuff."

He was in good humor, now that he was on the right side of the manuscript. Even the mouse I had planted under his eye didn't seem to bother him. He rubbed his hands and went back to work with the cuttings, correcting or qualifying Naharro's translations first. He didn't have Naharro's reference books and didn't seem to need them. Occasionally a word would stump him, but he put it aside and went on to the next, saving the doubtful one until he could study it in context.

I watched him for a while, yawning. I had had a full day. He finally said, "I'll be working on these all night. Why don't you go back to the hotel and get some sleep? One of us has to get up early and find out when the train leaves for Cuzco. I can work on your prints on the train, and it won't hurt to let Naharro know you've pulled out—say, for Lima, or some other place that isn't Cuzco."

"It's an idea. I'll see you in the morning."

I started for the door. Without looking up from his

work, he said, "How about my gun?"

"I feel safer with it."

"Safer from what?"

"Everything."

"Get one of your own, then."

"I like yours."

I left him with that to think over and went down the rickety staircase and out through the dark garden to where the hunchbacked *concerje* crouched in his gunnysack, shivering with cold, by the gate. He would sit there all night, every night, to earn five or ten *soles* a week—unless he was another *criatura*, and got only the rice for his belly and the gunnysack to keep himself warm. I wondered if he knew that his ancestors had worn golden crowns and called themselves sons of the sun.

It surprised me to see Raul in the *cantina* at the hotel. Julie was with him, still sober, as far as I could tell, which was even more strange. That they were together didn't mean anything, because two people like that would come together like two raindrops, wherever they met. But Raul should be having more important work to do than buying *limonadas* for a *gringa*.

I realized that he was there to keep an eye on me, see what I would do next. That made it easy. I told the clerk that I was leaving the next day for Mollendo, by train, and to call me early. As I slunk past the *cantina*, I was careful not to meet their eyes.

Julie laughed at my beaten-down look, a loud, long, mocking laugh that followed me up the stairs.

12

Raul couldn't follow me around town, of course. But don Ubaldo wasn't taking any chances. There was another man on my tail when I left the hotel in the morning. He was a young *cholo,* not very good at the job. I had him spotted before I had gone two blocks.

He followed me to the railroad station, where I bought a ticket for Mollendo. The day's train had already gone, and the next one left the following morning. I didn't have to ask questions about anything else, because a schedule was posted beside the ticket window. A day train for Juliaca and Cuzco left in one hour.

It would have to be cut fine, but it could be done. The *cholo* missed the *camioneta* I caught grinding up the hill toward town, not because I tried to lose him but because he wasn't on his toes. I dropped off at the bank, got my girl-show magazine out of hock, and slipped it inside my shirt in the manager's office while I was using his telephone.

Jeff's voice sounded dopey when I got him on the line. I said, "Make any progress?"

"Not much. I finished what can be done. Where are you?"

"At the bank. The train leaves for Cuzco in an hour. I had company, so I bought a ticket to Mollendo. Get down to the station and buy two tickets. Better make them second-class, and get on the train early to hold the seats."

"O.K. What kind of company did you have?"

"An amateur. I've already lost him, but he may pick me up again. If anything goes wrong, I'll meet you in Cuzco."

"O.K. Ask for Tacho Peralta's house, near the fortress."

My *cholo* was waiting for me at the hotel when I got there. If I'd had the time, I would have liked to give him a couple of lessons. He was leaning against a tree in the *parque* opposite the hotel, reading a newspaper. Instead of having the paper folded into a manageable size around whatever he was reading, he held it open in front of his face, like a woman hanging up washing. I suppose he had bored a hole through the paper so he could watch what was going on. His arms must have ached.

Nobody I knew was in the lobby or the *cantina*. I told the clerk that I had missed the Mollendo train, but that I would be taking the next one, early the following morning, and would pay in advance for the day so I could clean up my account and not have to waste time at the last minute. The *cholo* was still hanging up washing while I packed my bag, carried it down the back stairway and through the kitchen, out behind the hotel to where the road coming up from town made a sweeping circle short of the desert barrier marked by the irrigation ditch, looped the hotel, and started back where it came from. I was on the first *camioneta* that came around the circle. I could have reached out the window and knocked the *cholo's* hat over his eyes as we went by, but I didn't.

I made the train with ten minutes to spare. Jeff flipped his hand at me from the window of one of the second-class carriages. He had two seats that he was holding only because he looked too tough to argue with. The train was already full, Indians and *cholos,* mostly, with a few shabby white collars and a couple of priests in their heavy wool *sutanos.* The car stank with the smell that exists only on the desert side of Peru, where the population is heavy and water is too valuable to waste on washing. It was a dead, rancid smell that even the breeze from the open windows wouldn't blow away.

Jeff said irritably, "What was the idea of going second class? We'll have eight or nine hours of this stink before we reach Juliaca."

"We'll change there. Naharro will check up to see that I'm on the Mollendo train tomorrow. When he learns that I'm not, he'll ask around. He'll expect me to travel first class, and he may waste enough time to give us another day's leeway. We'll need it."

"We'll earn it, too." Jeff moved closer to the open window. "Give me the print."

I gave him one print. The other was inside the lining of my suitcase, for emergencies. His gun was in my hip pocket, also for emergencies. I hoped that he wouldn't make me use either of them.

He worked all day on the translation, humped over in his corner of the seat with a suitcase balanced on his knees, but he made no real progress because he kept falling asleep. I had to shake him awake half a dozen times. He had been up most of the night, working on the cuttings I had left with him, and the change in altitude knocked him out as effectively as a pill. The climb was terrific. The rattletrap train chugged and growled its way up out of the desert and across mile after bare mile of rocky, rolling *puna,* the high grassland of the Andean *altiplano,* twisting back and forth along grades that called for every ounce of steam in the engine's leaky boiler. I couldn't let Jeff sleep. Naharro would be close behind us, for one thing, and for another I had to know if three pieces of parchment out of the middle of the manuscript were enough to take us somewhere or just a tantalizer. I hadn't forgotten that Berrien, who knew his business, had paid five thousand dollars for them. But with the fever on me, I had to know what it was he had bought.

Whenever he could stay awake, Jeff copied his translations from the cuttings to the whole print, tearing the cuttings into shreds and tossing the shreds out the window. He had finished with the cuttings and was scowling at what he had on the print when I asked him for the fourth or fifth time if he was making any progress.

"We get something," he said.

"What? How much? Where is it?"

"I can't tell yet. The stuff was hidden in batches. This part of the manuscript covers an inventory of one batch, directions for finding a second inventory, and something over."

"Are the directions for the second batch complete?"

"Looks like it. Shut up and leave me alone."

I left him alone. I didn't even wake him after he fell asleep again, because the *soroche,* the mountain sickness, got me. My ears were ringing like doorbells when we reached the pass at Crucero Alto, fifteen thousand feet up, a bare, windswept, chilly clutch of huts in a shallow valley where even the herds of llamas feeding along the tracks huddled together for warmth and company. I had been living too long in the lowlands to make the change easily. My head ached, my arms and legs were like lead, I could barely see for the spots that danced in front of my eyes. If Jeff had been awake to notice what shape I was in, see how easy it would have been to take the gun from me, yank me off the train and knock me over the head behind the nearest snowdrift, things would have worked out differently for both of us. But he slept on, and after we passed the peak and started down, I snapped out of it.

He finished the job in a grimy *pensión* in Juliaca, where we had dinner. We were still on the *altiplano*, better than two miles high, and the air was so cold that I bought mittens and a muffler from an Indian woman at the railroad station and wore them while I ate. Jeff hardly touched his food. All through dinner he cursed and muttered over the last few knots that still held the puzzle together. He was jittery from fatigue and gold-fever, and his jitters infected me. Before he finished, I was hanging over his shoulder, watching the message grow, word by word. It wasn't only the altitude that made my breath come short and hard when I saw what was written on those three pieces of four-hundred-year-old *pergamino*.

This is how they read:

> "...*plate from the Hall of the Rainbow to the extent of fifty* arrobas; *six heavy vases of gold embossed with*

serpents; silver in bars, unworked; statues of the llama, in gold and silver; golden footwear and mantles of gold beads from the House of the Virgins of the Sun; other gold and silver ware. All this from the report of Huetín, who was put to the torture afterward by the Spaniards and died without speaking."

"The fourth. Beneath a boulder in the bed of the River of Amarú, eighty-four finely wrought pieces from the garden of the Temple of the Sun, including images of the llama, the vicuna and the alpaca, in gold; images of the maize plant, in gold and silver; images of the quinua plant, in gold; images of the sun, in gold, and the moon, in silver; flower pieces of gold with emeralds and turquoise; images of snakes, lizards and birds, in gold. The boulder, which is shaped like an egg erect on its large end, lies at a distance of one thousand varas toward the south from the southernmost point of the outer wall of the fortress of Sacsahuamán, and must be toppled away from the stream bed, after first cutting the hillside away to permit its fall and then removing a keystone at its base. All this from the report of Zaran, who was afterward put to the torture by the Spaniards and died without speaking."

Jeff's voice cracked at the end. I licked my lips. My mouth was dry.

"Just like that," I said foolishly. "Eighty-four pieces. What's the rest of it?"

Jeff read:

"The fifth. In a chamber beneath the second wall of

the fortress of Sacsahuamán, many large objects too cumbersome to remove before the arrival of the Spaniards, including large ceremonial vessels from the Temple of the Sun, in gold; statues of the Incas, in gold..."

Jeff threw the paper at me with an angry sweep of his arm.

"And that's all," he snarled. "What a haul we'd make with the next sheet of parchment! The statues of the Incas! Do you know what that means?"

I knew what it meant. It meant that Prescott's story hadn't been just another fairy tale. It meant that Don Carlo's lady had seen what she claimed to have seen— fourteen statues, each the size of a twelve-year-old boy, all of massive gold! Fourteen tons of gold in the statues alone, not including large ceremonial vessels from the Temple of the Sun, and other objects too cumbersome to move!

I ran my hand over my face. It came away wet.

"Where is the fortress of Sacsahuamán?" I said.

"Right above Cuzco, on a hill. The Spaniards wrecked it for building stone."

"Then they probably found the room with the statues in it."

"Not if it's under the wall. Some of the stones are as big as freight cars. They couldn't budge them. And there's no record of a discovery like that. If we could hit *that* one..."

Jeff smacked his hands together.

"We've got to find the rest of the parchment, that's all. Are you sure Berrien didn't have it?"

"He didn't take it out of Chile."

"Then we've got to go back to Chile. We've got to talk to the *hacendado* who sold it, and trace it back. Even with one more page…"

"The first thing we've got to do is get those eighty-four pieces out from under that rock. Naharro isn't going to wait. Tomorrow morning, when he learns that I didn't take the Mollendo train, he'll be right on our tail. How far is it from here to Cuzco?"

"The *nocturno* train leaves here at nine o'clock. We'll get in at seven or eight."

"How fast can Naharro follow us—by plane, say?"

"He can't. The plane comes direct from Lima. He could make it in a day and a night by hard driving, if the roads are in shape."

"Then we've got a clear day and a half to count on—with luck."

Jeff nodded. He watched me without a word while I picked up the print with his translation on it, folded it, and put it in my pocket.

"One thousand *varas* south of the south wall of the fortress of Sacsahuamán, under an egg-shaped boulder," I said. "Half for you, half for me."

He nodded again, slowly.

"We'd better see about catching the *nocturno*."

He nodded again.

We left the *pensión* and trudged back to the railroad station in a biting wind that swept across the barren *puna* to chill our bones. We didn't talk any more. And when the *nocturno* pulled out for Cuzco, we slept in separate compartments.

That was my idea. I suppose I was getting old, but it was a dirty racket, and the arithmetic was simple: eighty-four divided by two is forty-two, eighty-four divided by one is eighty-four.

I didn't want to shoot Jeff if a locked door between us made it unnecessary.

13

The *nocturno* was late getting into Cuzco. At nine o'clock the train was still winding down a pretty, well-watered valley laid out in garden patches and pastures where cattle and sheep grazed side by side with llamas and alpacas. The Incas had picked a good place to establish their capital. There on the eastern slope of the Andes, the bare *puna* had given way to a fertile country of hills and rivers, high enough to be above the jungle and yet below the frost line of the snow-capped peaks surrounding it. The rock terraces with which the Incas had lined the hillsides were still under cultivation, row after row climbing the steep mountain sides up to the snow-pack that gave them irrigation and brought life to the valley.

I had plenty of time to look at the scenery. Jeff and I hadn't said ten words to each other since leaving Juliaca. I knew how the arithmetic was going on in his head. He was a crook himself, and because he was a crook he had to figure me the same way. From his viewpoint, the only logical thing to do was to beat me out of

my share before I beat him out of his. All I wanted to do
was get the stuff, get rid of it, give him his cut, and
brush him off, but there was no way to convince him
that I was on the level. I was in the position of a man
who knows he is going to be slugged and can't slug first.
It was hard on the nerves.

When the train puffed into the little station at Cuzco,
he spoke for the first time that morning.

"We'd better split up. Naharro knows by now that
you didn't take the train to Mollendo, and he may have
a spotter here. We don't want to be seen together."

"We don't want to get too far apart, either."

He didn't pretend to misunderstand me. He said,
"I've got to round up burros and tools. I'll meet you at
Tacho Peralta's shack, across town on the slope below
the fortress. Ask your way. If I don't show up for a
couple of hours, don't get excited."

He picked up his bag and swung off the train on the
side away from the station.

I didn't have to reach for my bag. A *cholo* climbed in
through the window of the train before it stopped and
beat another *cholo,* who had used the door, to the bag
by a nose. The first *cholo* had a banged-up Ford parked
outside the station. He drove me up to town and
through narrow, cobbled streets that almost shook my
liver loose, pointing out the remains of Inca palaces and
temples with one hand while he slammed the horn with
the other. He had his mind on a big tip from the *gringo*
tourist. This was the Street of the Seven Snakes, and
that was the Palace of Inca Yupanqui, and over there
was the wall of the Temple of the Sun, whiz-bang

through the alleys so fast that all I saw was the soft-drink signs over the century-old stone doorways. Two hundred thousand people had lived in Cuzco during the days of the Incas, according to the *cholo*. There were about twenty thousand left, from the smell, plus a lot of llamas. It had rained there during the night, and now the sun shining on the muddy cobbles raised a stink that was terrible. The Indians on the street were dirty, undersized and ragged. Scrawny dogs and rickety kids were everywhere. It was hard to imagine Cuzco as it had been once, a city of kings, blazing with gold and jewels.

The *cholo* thought I was crazy when I told him to take me to Tacho Peralta's house. He knew where it was, but I had to repeat the name twice before he would drive me there instead of to the tourist hotel. Was I sure I didn't have Tacho mixed up with somebody else?

I said I was sure. He gave up building himself a tip and dumped me off at the last of a straggle of huts that climbed a steep hill at the far edge of town.

I could see why he had wondered if I knew what I was doing. Tacho's hut was made of mud, with a thatched roof. A mud wall crowned with spikes of growing cactus shut it off from the road. There was no gate, just a gap in the wall that led into a small, dirty yard where chickens pecked aimlessly. A couple of mangy dogs came yapping and snarling at my ankles. I kicked them away, kicked them away again, and slipped the belt out of my pants when they made a third try.

Their howls brought a skinny Indian in a *poncho* out

of the hut. He had the empty face and cloudy eyes of a *coca* chewer. The wad of leaf in his mouth bulged his cheek. Even from a distance I could see the louse nits in his greasy hair.

I said, "Are you Tacho Peralta?"

"Who wishes to know?"

"A friend of Señor Jefferson."

"I am Tacho."

He waited for me to say something else, if I felt like it. He wasn't curious. All that mattered to him was the cud in his mouth.

I said, "He asked me to wait for him here. I came with him on the train."

The Indian let it seep in for a minute. His jaws moved. Finally he said, "Enter."

I picked up my bag and followed him.

I wished I hadn't as soon as I got inside. The hut was as dirty as he was. There was no floor, only bare earth. A woman sat in a corner nursing a baby. She looked up indifferently when I came in. Her exposed breast was dirty, spotted with rash.

Tacho said, "Go away."

She got up, supporting the baby in the crook of her arm, and left the hut without a word. Tacho said, "Sit down."

I took the bench the woman had been sitting on. It was the only piece of furniture in the hut, except for a water *olla* and a bed cluttered with a huddle of smelly *ponchos*. Tacho leaned against the wall.

It took him five minutes to dredge up a sentence.

"Don Cheff sent no message."

"Don Jeff will be here soon."

We waited. When the smell of the place got to be too much for me, I went out into the chicken-littered yard and looked at what I could see of Cuzco: tile roofs, corrugated iron and church towers. Tacho followed me, chewing his *coca*. From his skinny bare ankles and wrists, he had been on the stuff a long time. You don't need to eat when you chew *coca,* or drink much either, or think, or do anything else. You just chew.

It must have been two hours before Jeff showed up, although it seemed longer. He was driving three furry burros with rawhide packsaddles on their backs. Strapped across one of the packsaddles were shovels, a pick and a crowbar.

He kicked the burros through the gap in the mud wall. Tacho picked up their trailing nose-ropes and tied their heads to their ankles to hobble them.

Jeff said, "Tacho, we will sleep here tonight. Where is your woman?"

"I sent her away."

"Find her and tell her to buy food." Jeff gave him a handful of *soles*. "Meat, rice, tea. A bottle of *pisco*. Have her clean the hut."

Tacho looked at the money in his hand, then at Jeff again, waiting. Jeff gave him another couple of *soles*. He closed his hand over the money and slouched away.

I said, "You can sleep in there if you want to. Too many lice for me."

"We've got to keep under cover, and this is the best place to do it. We'll be gone before dawn."

"What's your idea?"

"Find the boulder today. Knock it over before sun-up tomorrow, when nobody will see us working."

"Does Tacho know enough to keep his trap shut?"

"He's all right. He's done jobs for me before. You don't have to worry about him."

I thought: I'm not worried about Tacho. All I said was, "When do we start?"

"As soon as he gets back."

Tacho was back in fifteen minutes. The road past his house led on up the hill where I knew the fortress to be. I couldn't see the fortress, but the hill wasn't high. I had climbed steeper hills before. When Jeff told Tacho to strip the packsaddles off the burros and fix pads for riding, I looked at the animals' bony backs and said, "Why don't we walk?"

"A lot of reasons. Climbing at this altitude is hard on the heart, unless you're used to it. And we're both too big to pass as Indians, on foot. A couple of *gringos* nosing around the ruins would attract too much attention."

"You think you'll look like an Indian on a burro?"

"If I didn't know what I was doing, I wouldn't be doing it."

He went into the hut.

When he came out, he carried an armful of *ponchos* and a couple of *chullos*, the knitted caps with ear-tabs that the *altiplano* Indians wear. He gave me a *poncho* and a *chullo*. They both smelled as if dogs had been sleeping on them. But when we had slipped our heads through the neck-slits in the *ponchos* and pulled the *chullos* down over our ears, I could see that he did know what he was doing. Only somebody who got close enough to notice our shoes would have known that we were anything but a couple of Quechuas.

"Sit back on the burro's rump, the way an Indian does," Jeff said shortly. "Ready?"

"Let's go."

We rode single file up the road, Tacho jogging along in front, Jeff behind him. I stayed in the rear. The burros were just barely big enough so that my feet didn't drag, but they got us up the hill. It was the middle of the day, *siesta* time. We didn't meet anyone, except for a station wagon full of tourists going back toward town. One of the tourists snapped a picture of the three picturesque Indians on their donkeys as we pulled aside to let the car pass. The road looped back and forth a couple of times and came out on a level hilltop where the ruins of the fortress of Sacsahuamán huddled like a crouching dog watching over the town below.

The fortress had been pretty well wrecked. Only the largest stones remained. I could see why the *conquistadores* hadn't bothered with them. Some of them must have weighed fifty tons. They were irregularly shaped, but squared off and fitted together smoothly all around like a jigsaw puzzle, if you can imagine a jigsaw puzzle with pieces the size and weight of box cars. We had come up on the north side of the ruin, and as we rode along the outer wall I saw what a tremendous job it had been to make that fort what it was once. You couldn't have wedged a pin in the joints between the stones. There was no mortar. The joints were only lines marking the juncture of perfectly matched pieces of rock, fitted together so tightly that even the rain of centuries hadn't been able to seep in and separate them. Inside the outer wall was a second and a third, as tight and well-built as the first. Inside the third wall was a mound of rubble and grassy earth, nothing more.

Half to himself, Jeff said, "Under the second wall. It might be within twenty yards of us right now! If we had a case of dynamite…"

"If we had a case of dynamite, we'd blow ourselves right off this hill and into the jug. Stick to what we have, and don't talk like a fool!"

He almost fired back at me, not quite. We were both on edge.

We took our direction from the sun. It was noon. Tacho, who did the pacing, started in the longest shadow cast by the outer wall of the fortress and struck off down the hill, going away from town. Jeff and I kept to our burros and the road, which wandered away in a southerly direction. Below us, in a shallow valley planted with wheat, a stream flowed toward the hill on which the fortress stood, made a right angle toward the west, skirted the base of the hill, and curved off toward town. Tacho's straight path down the hill touched the stream at the bend. But he didn't stop there. He kept going, drawing farther and farther away from the stream-bed into the green wheat.

Jeff said nervously, "The direction must be off."

We were jogging down the road, kicking the burros into a bumpy trot to cover the mile or so of curves which Tacho was shortcutting in a straight line. I said,

"The direction is all right by the sun. What does a *vara* mean to Tacho?"

"A yard. A short pace and a half."

"It could be less. A *vara* doesn't have to be a yard."

"I know it. But it wouldn't be less than two and a half feet, and even that would take him past the stream. Something is wrong."

"Can he count?"

"I'm counting for him. Shut up!"

Tacho was still plodding on through the wheat, angling across a shallow swale that sloped down the far side of the little valley. The wheat was divided into small patches by irrigation ditches and low rock walls that he jumped or climbed without changing his direction. He was in the middle of a patch that lay a good two hundred yards from the stream-bed when Jeff whistled.

Tacho stopped. There wasn't a boulder near him, nothing but a solid checkerboard of green wheat-patches rippling in the wind.

The road crossed the bottom of the swale and looped away out of sight over the shoulder of the hill above it. The little valley slept quietly in the sun. Nobody was in sight. We left the burros at the side of the road and waded through the knee-high wheat to where Tacho stood.

Jeff said again, "The direction is off."

"Not more than a few yards. The nearest point of the stream is just about southwest of the fortress. Are you sure the manuscript said south?"

"Yes."

"Then it's our distance."

"Even if we cut the *vara* down to two and a half feet, it still leaves us in the wheat. There isn't a boulder in sight, or a stream—unless you count rock fences and irrigation ditches."

Jeff yanked angrily at the ear-tabs of his *chullo*.

I said, "Let's stretch the *vara* out, then. Let's follow the ditches and see where they come from."

We left Tacho where he was and followed the ditches up the swale. Two hundred paces farther on, at the top of the slope, there was an irrigation sluice from which water ran down into the ditches in the wheat patches. The sluice was a rock-lined trough, full of slow-running muddy water.

I said, "The rock-work looks old enough to be Inca. Could the word have been translated 'sluice' or 'ditch' instead of 'stream'?"

"It could have been. If that's it, we're beat. There aren't any boulders here either."

Jeff scowled, sighting along the straight line of the sluice. It came down from somewhere up above, cutting across the top of the swale to empty finally into the stream which turned away below the fortress toward the town—the stream which should have been due south of the fortress but which flowed from the southwest and was fed by a sluice coming from the southeast.

Something about the sharp line that the sluice cut across the upper edge of the green wheat fields made me think of the irrigation ditch that brought water and life to Arequipa. I walked twenty yards up the hill and saw the answer.

Jeff was still standing there, scowling, when I came

back. I said, "They moved the stream. They sidetracked it up above and ran a sluice along the crest here so they could plant the creek bottom. Our distance was right. It's down below."

Jeff grunted. "I don't see any boulder."

"I don't either. But I'm not going to quit until I've made sure it isn't there."

It was there. It took us half an hour to find it. At the joining of two of the rock walls that separated the wheat into patches, not more than fifty feet from the point at which Tacho had stopped his pacing, the cornerpost was a smooth, rounded stone growing from the earth. The ground had silted up around it, after years of irrigation to bring water and soil down from above, so that it was pretty well buried. But it was in the bottom of the swale, where the stream had flowed four centuries before. And its rounded peak still pointed at the sky. The egg was still balanced on its heavy end.

Somebody—I don't know whether it was Jeff or me—let out his breath in a long sigh. That was all. We replaced the stones we had taken from the wall to make sure we were on the right track, and went back to where the burros were munching mouthfuls of stolen wheat.

A guide was taking another party of tourists through the fortress when we plodded by, the *ponchos* high around our necks to hide our faces. I heard him telling the tourists of a legend about fourteen solid-gold statues buried somewhere beneath their feet. He laughed as he told it, and the tourists laughed with him. They were too grown-up for fairy stories.

I thought a lot about those statues during the afternoon. We stayed under cover in Tacho's hut, waiting for time to pass. There wasn't anything for us to talk about. We were in a kind of state of suspended animation, wound up like alarm clocks, waiting for the hour hand to reach a certain point and trip the release that would set us off. I could feel the tight spring coiled inside me. The burros in the yard switched their tails at flies and nuzzled the short grass growing between the cobbles. When night came at last, Tacho's woman turned up from somewhere carrying a blackened five-gallon kerosene can. She made a fire in the can inside the hut. There was no chimney, and the smoke hung thickly at shoulder height, but even then the hut was cold. A chill had come into the air as soon as the sun went down. I was grateful for the smelly *poncho* and the *chullo* to pull down over my ears.

I learned, that night, why a *poncho* is made the way it is, with a slit for your head and no sleeves. You can scratch yourself without exposing your arms to the cold. Jeff's *poncho* was either cleaner than mine or he was more accustomed to lice than I was, because he scratched about half as often. But even Tacho, who must have been solid scar tissue from bites, pawed himself once in a while. We squatted on the bare dirt around the fire-can, our heads an inch below the smoke-level, and scratched, while Tacho's woman boiled a chicken with rice and made tea.

She never said a word. Neither did we. Once the baby the woman carried slung across her back in a dirty *rebozo* began to yell. The woman looked frightened. I don't know why, unless she could feel the tension stretching between Jeff and me across the fire, and was afraid of breaking it. She pulled the baby around in front and let it suck while she served us food. Afterward she brought in armloads of wood for the fire and then disappeared.

I never want to spend another night like that one. Neither Jeff nor I slept. We squatted on either side of the fire-can, huddled in our *ponchos,* moving only to stretch our legs or scratch. Tacho dozed, waking occasionally to throw more wood into the can. Once he scraped a handful of ashes from the coals to mix with a fresh wad of *coca*. It was his food, drink, blanket, bed and family. It sustained him the way gold-fever was sustaining Jeff and me. We never relaxed for a second. The light from the fire was just enough to let me see Jeff's eyeballs shining unwinkingly. I knew his thoughts as well as he thought he knew mine, the same old simple arithmetic: eighty-four divided by two is forty-two, eighty-four divided by one is eighty-four.

The night wore on, colder and colder, hour after hour. The burros stamped and snorted with cold outside the hut. Jeff watched me, I watched him, we waited. His gun made a lump in my belt. The only thing that really worried me was the fact that I couldn't remember how long it had been since I had had typhus shots. The lice were pretty bad. If there was a rat louse mixed in with the others, it would be a poor joke to die with forty-two pieces of Inca gold on my hands. Eighty-four divided by two is forty-two, eighty-four divided by one is eighty-four.

Jeff's eyes glittered as the fire flared in the can. I

shifted the gun to a more comfortable position. Time passed.

A cock flapped his wings five times somewhere outside, the beats as loud as handclaps in the still, cold air, and crowed. Another cock answered from half a mile away. A third, farther off, picked it up, and the *¡quiquiriquí!* went off across the countryside, cock answering cock until the sound was a whisper in the distance.

Jeff said, "Tacho!"

The Indian grunted and came awake. Jeff said, "What time is it?"

Tacho sniffed the air. The cock crowed again, with the same preliminary loud beat of its wings. One of the burros brayed, complaining at the cold.

"Two," Tacho said.

"We'd better get started," Jeff said to me. "We'll have to finish the digging before light."

I creaked to my feet. My legs were as stiff as boards until I stamped the circulation back into them. Jeff and I silently ate what was left of the boiled chicken, handing the pot back and forth and scooping with our fingers. Tacho's breakfast was a fresh wad of *coca* leaf and wood ash.

Jeff wiped his greasy hands on his *poncho* when he finished eating.

"I'm driving now, whether you like it or not," he said curtly. "This is my racket. I'll tell you what to do and when to do it. If anything goes wrong, it's every man for himself."

"Fair enough. But don't let anything go wrong."

Because I was tired of the silent cutthroat game we had been playing, and wanted to bring it out in the open, I took the gun from under my *poncho* and examined it in the light from the fire-can. It was a .38, double action. There was one empty chamber in the cylinder. I tried the trigger-pull on the empty. The hammer came back easily and slipped smoothly off cock. It was a gunman's gun, made for business. I slipped it back inside my belt.

"I'm ready, any time," I said.

Jeff said something. It may have been a curse. I saw his lips move, but I didn't hear the words because one of the burros in the yard brayed again as a packsaddle hit his back. Tacho was saddling up.

It was bitterly cold outside. The moon had gone down, but the stars were like lanterns. In the east, Venus glowed so brightly that she cast a shadow. A few street lights burned in the city. Above us, the hill of the fortress was a black curtain against the stars. We straddled the burros' rumps, behind the packsaddles, and kicked them out through the gap in the mud wall. Tacho's burro carried the tools, clinking metallically in the darkness.

Once we had started, the minutes seemed to pass quickly. We jogged up the hill, past the dark bulk of the ruined fortress, and down the winding road into the shallow valley where the wheat grew. The irrigation ditches were still running. This time we took the burros with us, over rock walls and ditches to where the job was to be done. Tacho, by smell or by instinct, led us straight to the egg-shaped rock.

"All right," Jeff said. "Let's work fast. Tacho, clear these stones away. Colby, start digging on that side. I'll take this one."

I pulled the *poncho* off over my head, shivered at the bite of the cold air, and reached for a shovel.

I wasn't cold for long. The ground was soft and spaded easily, but the bottom land had silted up until two-thirds of the boulder was buried. We had to cut the slope down five feet to reach the keystone. I found it with my fingers, a tapering wedge of rock. There was no mistaking it, even in the dark. The cut edges were as smooth and straight as the sides of a wedge of cheese.

"I've got the keystone." My heart was thumping, partly from the effort of digging at that altitude, partly from something else. "It's tight. It will have to be knocked loose."

"We've got to clear a space for the rock to fall, first."

We dug for another hour before the pit was ready. It had to be long enough and deep enough to take the full mass of the boulder when it fell, because if the base didn't clear whatever it covered when we toppled it, there would be nothing to do but dig a new pit. And the sky was growing gray in the east.

Tacho dug like a machine. Without his *poncho* he was as thin as a skeleton, except for the big chest of the high-altitude native, yet he moved more earth than Jeff or I. The *coca* gave him energy without intelligence to go with it. He had to be told where to dig, and when to stop. He was an animal, like one of the burros munching wheat at the edge of the pit, but without him we would never have finished the job before daylight. As it was, there was enough light in the sky for us to see each other clearly when at last the pit was finished and the base of the boulder cleared of dirt.

The stone was eight feet high, almost perfectly egg-shaped. Seen in the clear, it was balanced slightly off vertical, the center of gravity away from what had been the stream bed, so that an attempt to push it over into the stream, the natural way to try to move it, would have stalled a bulldozer. The keystone on the opposite side acted as a wedge to hold it from going the other way.

Somebody had to get down in the pit to knock the keystone loose. I picked up the crowbar, intending to give it to Tacho. It would be too easy for Jeff to slam me over the head with a spade while I worked. But he grabbed the crowbar from me.

"I'll do it." He was breathing hard. "You've got the gun, and it's light enough for some of these Indians to be taking a look at their ditches. Get up on top and keep a lookout."

I didn't move. He said angrily, "Damn it, we've gone too far to let anybody interfere with us now! If you're afraid to use the gun, give it to me."

"I'll use the gun any time I have to."

"Then get up there on top—and stop anybody who comes too close!"

He jumped down into the pit.

I don't know if I would have used the gun in a pinch. I might have. The fever was pretty hot. I squatted in the dew-wet wheat above the pit while Jeff worked with the crowbar down below. Both he and Tacho were out of sight. I was nearly hidden by the wheat, and there was nothing particularly strange about three stray burros in a field. Several Indians, shapeless in their *ponchos,* passed along the road without noticing anything out of the ordinary. Stars faded as the light grew brighter in the sky. I smelled the heavy loaminess of turned earth, the stink of burro, the rich greenness of growing wheat, and gold, gold, gold! It was as strong as the odor of blood. My heart pounded in my chest.

The crowbar came up out of the pit. Jeff followed it, panting. He hauled Tacho up behind him.

"Got it," he said. "Come on."

The three of us put our weight against the far side of the boulder. It rocked, came back, rocked again, came back…

"*¡Ya!*" I dug in my toes.

Jeff's muscles cracked. Tacho grunted. The boulder balanced, swayed, and went into the pit, exposing a rectangular base, perfectly flat, except for the groove cut for the keystone, and mortised to fit the cavity below as neatly as if it had been cast in a mold. The cavity itself, cut from solid bedrock, was full to the brim of smooth, undisturbed sand.

I think even Tacho swore. I dropped to my knees and began to paw the sand like a dog, forgetting Jeff, the gun, everything. Jeff was beside me, making noises in his throat. My fingers hooked something. I heaved, got another grip, and came up with a heavy, hammered disc the size of a dinner plate, crusted with the oxidization of four centuries but still with enough glitter left to wink dully in the first rays of the sun peeking over the mountains, sun winking at sun.

14

We took ninety-three pieces out of the hole, instead of eighty-four. Jeff's translation had been off somewhere. They weighed over three hundred pounds, at a guess. The hole was five feet long, a yard deep, and two and a half feet wide, full of fine sand that had silted in through the hair-line crack around the base of the boulder. Gold, silver and jeweled metal filled the sand like potatoes. Tacho, the smallest man among us, got down in the hole and dug them with a spade. Once a couple of Indians coming up the road from town stopped to point at us and jabber, but they didn't come any closer. They must have smelled death in the air.

We worked fast, not even bothering to knock the sand out of hollow ware. There were extra *ponchos* on the packsaddles. The ninety-three pieces made three packs, with the *ponchos* for covering. The burros went right on snatching mouthfuls of wheat while we loaded them. They were starved, skinny beasts, covered with sores, and they were having the best feed of their lives. But we had to get them moving soon, because the town below us was waking up. More Indians were coming up the road.

I was fastening the last lashing of one of the packs. Jeff worked on another, Tacho a third. I said, "We have to get this stuff under cover before we get picked up for ruining some *cholo's* wheat patch."

"You won't have to worry about that," Jeff answered.

I looked up from the knot I was tying.

He had another gun. It pointed at me over the back of the two burros standing between us.

"Just finish the knot," he said. "You've given me a lot of trouble, smart guy. You're through now."

I tried to swallow, staring at the gun. But I was already dead. There wasn't anything in my mouth except dust.

Jeff grinned his wolf grin.

"You've got a stronger heart than Berrien," he said conversationally. "When I lifted him out of his bunk, he woke up and tried to yell. I put my hand over his mouth and he bit me, so I stuck the gun into his face and said, *"Los muertos no muerden, amigo Alfredo,"* letting the hammer come back slow—the way it's coming back now, smart guy—*adiós…"*

His finger cramped on the trigger. The hammer lifted. But the gun didn't have the easy pull he was used to, and the hammer was still going back toward cock when I kicked the burro, ducked, threw myself to one side, and reached for the pistol in my belt, all at the same time.

It was no good. Jeff's slug hit me like a baseball bat, high up in the shoulder, knocking me stumbling back on my heels. In the time it took me to go down, I heard a burro scream through the roar of the gun, saw the animals jump and scatter, heard Jeff shout. Tacho started toward me, but I wasn't around when he got there. I was falling, falling, falling…

*

A rectangle of bright sky hung over my head when I came back to earth. For a long time I couldn't figure out where I was. I seemed to be in a box of some kind, like an open coffin. The coffin was too small for me. I was all hunched up, my legs doubled over nearly to my chest. I tried to change my position and gave up the idea when broken bones scraped in my shoulder. The shock of the bullet had worn off by then. The wound throbbed and burned. There was a sticky warmness under my back, and something sharp that dug into my flesh.

I worked my good hand underneath me, inch by inch—I was pretty weak—and pulled out the thing that was digging me.

It was an image of a vicuña, about three inches high, the long snake-like neck curved down as if he were feeding, the ears flat against the narrow skull. I looked at it for a couple of minutes before it meant anything. Then I knew that I was in the treasure box, bleeding to death with a dirty chunk of solid gold in my hand.

Good joke on Jeff, I thought dimly. The parchment had said ninety-four pieces, not eighty-four.

I lay there, feeling light-headed and weak and thirsty, wondering how long it would take me to die, and thinking, sucker, sucker, sucker. You should have known he would find another gun. *Adiós,* smart guy. The stickiness under my back was spreading. My louse-bites itched. I scratched a couple I could reach, and thought how dumb it was to check out scratching louse-bites. It would be better to use the energy yelling. I tried it, but my head was cramped down against my chest and I didn't have enough steam left to raise more than a thin bleat. And when I got through bleating, I was too tired to scratch.

"Los muertos no muerden," Jeff had said. The dead don't bite. They don't itch, either, I thought. Have to make a noise, somehow. Where's the gun?

I couldn't find it in my belt. When I tried to paw around under my legs, the bones scraped in my shoulder and I passed out.

That was my last effort. Afterward I kept coming on and going off like a dim light, my thoughts getting hazier all the time until they were all concentrated in the throb of my shoulder. There was a lucid interval when I wondered why Jeff hadn't finished me off with another bullet, or cracked my skull with the crowbar if he was afraid of a second gunshot. Then I began to talk to the vicuña. We had a nice little conversation, all about gold and the fine taste of clear water. He sprouted a human head after a while, a pock-marked *cholo* face with a green traffic cop's helmet that hung over me with its mouth open and its eyes sticking out. I blinked at the face and made a clacking noise with my dry lips. The face blew up like a balloon.

The next person I saw was Ana Luz. She was feeding me water from a glass tube. She wore the white ribbon in her hair, just as she had when I first met her.

I was burning with fever, but I pushed the tube out of my mouth with my tongue and said foolishly, "What are you doing here? There isn't room for both of us."

"There's plenty of room. You're all right. Be quiet and drink."

She put the tube back in my mouth.

It tasted real. So did the water. I thought: At least I *think* I'm drinking, so I might as well enjoy it.

I took a couple of long pulls at the imaginary water and went to sleep.

My head was clear when I woke up the next time. I was in bed in a room that opened on a sunny *patio* full of flower bushes. A mimosa, bursting with yellow bloom, grew just outside the window. I could smell the blossoms. I could smell medicine, too, and my own body sweat. My left arm was locked up over my head in a cast that made me feel like the Statue of Liberty. I didn't hurt anywhere, except for a headache, but I was too weak to do any more than lie there and wonder why I wasn't dead.

Somebody said, "Hello."

I turned my head.

It was Julie. She put down the magazine she had been reading and came over to the bed. She didn't look bad at all, except for a drawn face. Somebody had taught her how to use make-up since the last time I saw her.

I said, "How did you get here? How did I get here? Where am I?"

"Cuzco. Don Ubaldo's house. Wait a minute."

She left the room. Waiting was all I could do, so I waited. Pretty soon she came back with Naharro.

He said, "How do you feel, Señor Colby?"

"Fine. How are you?"

"Very well. Do you feel strong enough to talk?"

"About what?"

166

"What we have always talked about."

He pulled up a chair and sat down, ignoring Julie. She stood there meekly, watching first my face and then Naharro's, trying to make something out of our Spanish.

Naharro said, "It will be best for you to guard your strength, so I will talk first for both of us. You and Jefferson arrived here five days ago. When you did not take the train to Mollendo, I had inquiries made at the station, learned where you had gone, and followed immediately by car. You had another photograph of the manuscript, which I had stupidly not considered, from which Jefferson made a translation. With that, you found the treasure. Either Jefferson or another man who was with him shot you. The burros on which the treasure was loaded stampeded at the shot, and by the time Jefferson and the other man had rounded them up, some Indians from the road were on hand to prevent them from coming back and finishing you off. They disappeared with the burros. You had either fallen or been thrown into the pit from which the treasure was taken. The Indians called a policeman from town in time to keep you from bleeding to death in the pit, but you were dying in the *clinica* here when I arrived. I wired for the best doctor in Lima, who flew here and saved your life. You have had a number of blood transfusions. Your collar bone and shoulder blade are broken, but the bones have been properly set. You are in my house in Cuzco, where I ask you to stay as my guest until you are fully recovered. Is there anything else I can tell you?"

"Many thanks. What am I to do for payment?"

"Help me to recover the treasure."

"You'll have to find Jefferson for that. All I got for my trouble was a three-inch gold vicuña—if it hasn't been stolen."

"The vicuña is safe. And we will find Jefferson, eventually. All the roads and trains are being watched, as well as the airfields. It will be difficult for a *gringo* of his size to disguise himself. But I am afraid that he may melt the metals down, to make their transportation easier, and the thought makes me sick to my soul, Señor Colby." Naharro blinked his lashless eyes at me. "He is a barbarian. I have had dealings with him before. Even Alfredo Berrien would have appreciated what you found for what it is. To Jefferson, it is so much gold and silver. Unless we can find him, and soon—I am afraid…"

He let it hang.

I said, "Who is watching the roads and trains?"

"The *guardia civil*."

"You told them?"

He nodded heavily.

"I told them. I will not say that I did not hope at one time to find the treasure myself. But rather than see it taken out of the country, melted down and lost forever to the world, like the spoils of the Conquest, I have informed the government. I ask your help to stop Jefferson before he can destroy it."

"How am I to help?"

"You must have made plans to smuggle it out of the country, some way. Where would he go?"

"My plans were to turn it over to the government for the discovery reward."

He frowned.

I said, "You can believe what you like."

"I cannot believe that Jefferson would agree to that, even if I accept your word. He would know how small the discovery reward is compared to the true value."

"It is clear that he had plans of his own."

"You do not know what they were?"

"I will have to think."

I closed my eyes. It wasn't only to shut him off. I was really tired, just from talking. After a minute, he said, "If anything occurs to you, all Peru will be grateful. But the time is short."

I heard him leave the room.

I was thinking: Across Lake Titicaca from Puno to Bolivia. Jeff had done it before, he could do it again. He must believe that he had killed me. All that stood between him and a fortune was a police cordon looking for a big *gringo* traveling by road, rail or plane. They'd never stop a couple of Indians with three burros, cutting across country to Puno. All they would do would be to make it necessary for Jeff to stick to the hills.

But that way, it would take him a week, maybe more. The train had taken nine hours to come from Juliaca to Cuzco, and Puno was on the other side of Juliaca. Say two hundred and twenty-five miles. With his starved, heavily loaded burros, Jeff couldn't make more than thirty or forty miles a day, however he drove them. And I wasn't afraid that he would melt the stuff down. Whatever Naharro thought of him, he knew the value of what he had.

I said, "How long did you say I had been here?"

I was talking to Naharro, forgetting that he had already left the room. Julie answered apologetically, "I'm sorry. My Spanish isn't very good. What did you say?"

I opened my eyes. She was still standing in the middle of the room, watching me.

I said, "What's the matter, haven't you got a knife handy? We're all alone."

She took it with her chin up.

"You're entitled to that, I suppose. But I wouldn't have wasted my own blood if I were going to use a knife on you."

She turned her arm over, showing me the patch of bandage below her elbow where the artery had been tapped.

I said, "Why?"

"I didn't want you to die."

"Why?"

"I know what you think of me, and I don't care. You did something awful to me that—that night in the hotel." She blinked quickly. "I wanted to get back at you, and I did, and when Raul told me that he and his father were following you to Cuzco I came back to see if I could do anything else to hurt you, but I never wanted you to die. And I think we're even now, so if you don't want anything more from me, like blood or—or something, I think I will go to Lima."

She was trying her best to make a good exit. It was too much for her. Her voice broke at the end. As she turned away, I said, "Wait a minute. Come over here and sit down."

She came to the bed and sat down, both hands over her face as they had been the night I showed her herself in the mirror.

I said, "I never thought you were a tramp, Julie. I think your sense of values is wrong, and you're pretty young to be kicking around on your own, but it takes more than that to make a tramp. I know I was brutal in Arequipa, but I was trying to show you something."

"You did." Her voice was muffled by her hands. "I haven't had a drink since. Not one."

"One or two or a dozen never hurt anybody, if you don't let it get away from you. If I were your father or your brother, I would have spanked your behind instead. That's all I meant by it, a spanking. If I did anything else to you, I'm sorry."

She took her hands away from her face, smiling tearfully.

"I guess I need a father or a brother or somebody. I never had anybody that I can remember, only too much money. I guess I'm pretty badly spoiled."

"You're all right. You're just headed in the wrong direction."

She wiped her eyes on her sleeve, like a child.

"What's the right direction for me?" she said, after a minute.

"I don't know. You have to work it out yourself. Some women get married and raise a family."

"I'd like a family. I'd like a big family, with aunts and uncles and babies and cousins all over the place. I haven't a relative in the world that I know of. Or even a good friend. Everybody I know…"

"Don't go around feeling sorry for yourself. Pick a good man with plenty of cousins and aunts and raise the rest yourself."

"I've picked him. It won't work."

"Why not?"

"It just won't, that's all." She stood up. "You're supposed to rest, and not talk so much. Is there anything you want? A—" she blushed "—bedpan or something?"

"No bedpan. I'd like to know who you've picked and why it won't work."

She shook her head. I said, "Get it off your chest."

She kept her mouth stubbornly shut. I said, "Come on."

She looked down at me for another minute before she gave in.

"Raul."

I wanted to laugh. I wanted to say, of all the men in the world... But I said, "Why him?"

"He's my type, I guess. I know you don't like him. He doesn't like you, either. But he likes me, and he's the kind of a man I need—I guess. Somebody to boss me around. You made me do a lot of thinking, after that night in the hotel. I was pretty miserable when he came along. At first he was only somebody I could use to get back at you, but then—I don't know what happened. Maybe I just needed somebody then worse than I ever had before. He was nice to me—I suppose because he wanted my help—it's hard to explain...."

"I know. You want to be bossed, and he likes to boss people. Why won't it work?"

"His father. He thinks I'm a—tramp, or whatever it is

in Spanish, and he wants Raul to marry Ana Luz. Raul doesn't want to marry her, and she doesn't want to marry him, and I want to marry him, and he wants to marry me, I think—or he would if I worked on him a little—but they have to do what his father says because Ana Luz is really his slave—his father's, I mean—and it's all so mixed up and hopeless it just isn't worth talking about. Now go to sleep, for Heaven's sake!"

She slammed out of the room.

I didn't go to sleep. I still had to figure the best way to stop Jeff. But I couldn't concentrate on Jeff and the treasure with Julie on my mind. I was sorry for her. She was a featherbrain, sure. But she wasn't as vicious as she was dumb, and she was just at the point where she could either go to the devil or turn into something, depending on how she was steered. Maybe Raul would be good for her. He wasn't any bargain, of course. Ana Luz was a million times too good for him. Ana Luz was the best one of the whole crew. But with don Ubaldo holding the reins...

My mind skipped around like that: gold, Jeff, Julie, Raul, Ana Luz, until I got an idea.

I suppose everyone likes to play at being God, one time or another. I played it that afternoon in Cuzco, the smell of sweat and medicine and mimosa in my nose, shuffling the lives of half a dozen people around the way you would shuffle a deck of cards, as helpless as a baby in my cast and at the same time as powerful as the grandest Inca that ever sat on a throne. Because I had the key to the Incas' gold, and you can buy a lot with gold, if you have enough of it—even new lives.

When I had it all figured out, I looked around for a bell.

There was a button in the wall near the head of the bed. I stretched for it with my good hand, knowing how a surgeon feels when he reaches for the knife. Only there wasn't any anesthetic for the job I intended to do.

15

Ana Luz came into the room. She was wearing the white dress and the white hair ribbon I had first seen her in. She stood silently in the doorway, like a good servant waiting for her orders.

I said, "I didn't expect you, but I'm glad you came. Will you sit down?"

"What do you want?"

"Five minutes of your time. Sit down."

She took the chair that was across the room, near the window where the mimosa bloomed. I said, "No, over here near me. I won't bite. I don't want to have to shout."

She brought the chair over to the bed and sat down, her hands folded in her lap.

I reached out and turned her left forearm over. There was a patch of bandage below the elbow joint.

I said, "You told me once that you were sorry we were enemies. I think we have stopped being enemies."

"The blood was nothing. We all gave some, except don Ubaldo, and he would have done it but for the doctor's refusal."

"Did you give me blood for the same reason that don Ubaldo would have given it—to keep alive the information that might be in my head?"

"I gave it because you were a dying man, and the blood was necessary."

"As you gave me water from a glass tube because I was feverish, and water was necessary?"

She nodded.

I said, "For that, I am going to give you what you want most."

A spark flashed into her eyes. It burned out quickly. She said, "It is not yours to give."

"I can buy it. First I want you to tell me how you came to be Alfredo Berrien's nurse."

She didn't answer. I said, "You begged me for the price of your freedom, once. You said you would do anything I asked. All I want is to know what you were to Berrien."

"A spy."

"For don Ubaldo."

"Yes."

"How did he get you the position?"

"Through an agency. He bribed them to put me at the head of the list when don Alfredo's former nurse left him. I had studied nursing in school."

"You reported to don Ubaldo what Berrien was doing, so don Ubaldo could rob him?"

"So that don Ubaldo could acquire things which don Alfredo would otherwise have acquired."

"Robbery is robbery, by any name."

She said wearily, "Call it what you like. If you are

trying to shame me, it is useless. May I go now?"

"No. Why did you send a radio message from the *Talca* to don Ubaldo, with my name in it?"

"Don Ubaldo wanted me to steal the manuscript which don Alfredo bought in Chile, and bring it to him. But I could not leave don Alfredo alone and helpless in Chile, and after he gave the manuscript to you there was nothing I could do. I sent the message to bring Raul to help me get it from you. He was angry that I had not stolen it when I had the chance—you saw us that night…"

"I remember. Does don Ubaldo know that his son slaps you?"

She shrugged indifferently.

"He expects you to marry Raul?"

"Yes."

"You will do as he expects?"

"He is my *patrón*."

"Does he know that Raul prefers the *gringa*?"

"Who can say?"

"You know it. You know that he would have her, or someone like her, for his *querida* after you were married. Yet you would still marry him, knowing this, because don Ubaldo wishes it?"

"He is my *patrón*."

That was her answer to everything. Don Ubaldo was her *patrón*. All her life it had been drilled into her. She was his *criatura*, to pass on, if he liked, to his son, like any other piece of property.

I said, "Did don Ubaldo promise you your freedom if you got the manuscript from Berrien?"

"I promised myself. It was something he wanted more than anything in the world. I felt that by making myself into a thief and a liar—perhaps even the cause of don Alfredo's death…"

"You were not the cause. Jeff frightened him to death."

"I am glad it was not the sleeping pills. But if I had got the manuscript for don Ubaldo, I would never have gone back." She smiled sadly. "You were more cruel than you knew, that afternoon in Lima."

"So because Raul, and not you, finally got it from me, you are not free?"

She nodded. It was very simple. She thought I was stupid not to see it.

"Bring don Ubaldo," I said.

She left the room obediently.

I looked at the ceiling until they came back. Ana Luz turned to go, but I stopped her.

"Wait. I want you to hear this. Don Ubaldo, how badly do you want to recover the treasure?"

"More than I want anything else."

"You hope to earn the discovery reward?"

"I hope to see the treasure in the museum in Lima, where it belongs. The reward means nothing to me. The treasure, yes. I would have given my soul to have made the discovery. Peru must have it—if it is not already too late."

"I think it is not too late. I think I know how to catch Jefferson. If I tell you, I want two things—the discovery reward and Ana Luz's freedom."

Naharro said coldly, "The discovery reward is paid by

the government. And I do not know what you mean by her freedom. She is already free."

"She is not free. She is your *criatura*."

"I do not like that word, señor. I have always looked on her as my daughter. She owes me no legal obedience since she became of age. But I do not see that our family affairs…"

I cut him off.

"I am entering into your family affairs. You expect her to marry your son. She does not want to, but she feels that she owes you something she has not been able to repay. She wants freedom, not the son of her *patrón* for a master. I will buy her freedom by recovering the treasure for you. Ana Luz, if he tells you that you are your own mistress, will it be enough?"

I thought she hadn't heard me, at first. Finally she nodded, her eyes on the floor.

Don Ubaldo said bitterly, "Are my home and my son so hateful to you then, *hija*?"

"Not hateful, believe me." She lifted her head. Her eyes glistened wetly. "I am grateful to you, don Ubaldo. More than I can say. But I do not want to marry Raul. I do not want to marry anyone. I want only to be as other people are, free to make my own life. Is it so much to ask?"

"I made you what you are," don Ubaldo said. "You were a starving beggar's child when I took you in. I raised you to be a lady, in the same way that I raised my own son to be a gentleman. Always I have planned that you two should marry, some day. For that day, you went to school, when you might have been tending sheep in the hills. You ate, when you might have been starving. You were sheltered and protected, and loved…"

"Like one of your son's horses!" There was fire in Ana Luz's voice now. "You made me into a gift for Raul, not a woman! You were kind to me, educated me, clothed and fed me—for Raul!"

"Never!"

"It's true! What kind of love do you speak of, who made me into a spy and a cheat for gold? What kind of love do you expect from me in return, for you or your son who looks on me as a servant to come when he claps his hands? Obedience—yes. I recognize the debt that I owe, and I will pay it as you like. I will marry Raul whenever you say. But I do not love him, or you, or what you have made of me. I would have been more grateful to you if you had let me starve!"

She dropped her head.

Don Ubaldo stood like a statue, his lips pressed tightly together. He had not looked at Ana Luz once.

I said, "Raul does not want to marry her, either. He loves the *gringa.*"

"The *gringa!*" He spat it out.

"Maybe Raul would like to be free, too. To some people, freedom is more important than all the treasure in the world, don Ubaldo. Your son means nothing to me. I think the *gringa* is too good for him. I know Ana Luz is too good for him. If you want the treasure recovered, tell her she is free."

Seconds ticked by. Don Ubaldo was like a stone. Beside him, Ana Luz began to tremble. Her hands knotted tightly.

"What is your interest in her?" don Ubaldo said.

"None. Perhaps I do this because she gave me her blood. Perhaps I am paying you for your dealings with me. Perhaps I do it only because I dislike you and your son. It is not important. If you feel as you tell me you feel about the treasure, you will do as I say."

His liverish face didn't change. In a flat, dead voice, he said, "You are free to do as you wish, Ana Luz. You are your own mistress."

I said, "And the discovery reward. You are a member of the National Institute of Archaeology. I want a pre-dated permit to dig, and your statement that I found the treasure first and was robbed of it."

In the same dead voice, Naharro said, "You will have the permit and my statement. Where will I find Jefferson?"

"I'll find him for you. Do you have a car here?"

"Yes."

"Get ready to leave in the morning for Puno. Let it be known that I am dead. It might be helpful if the news reached the woman of Tacho Peralta, an Indian who lives on the hill below the fortress. Tell the police to take the watch off the roads near Puno."

He turned away and left the room, his bald head erect, his back stiff.

Ana Luz took two quick steps and dropped to her knees beside my bed. Her lips trembled. She was trying to say something, without having the words to say it. I wanted to tell her that there was nothing she had to say, but I couldn't find the words myself. We looked at each other for a minute, both dumb, and then I felt her cool hands on my cheeks and her warm mouth on mine. Seconds later I was alone with the taste of her lips, feeling tired and triumphant and good.

16

We left for Puno in the morning.

The doctor that don Ubaldo had brought up from Lima had already gone back, so I never got a chance to thank him for saving my life. Another doctor was on hand to forbid me to get out of bed. He went right on forbidding me all the time I was getting dressed.

I was pretty shaky. Raul helped me with my clothes. He would rather have been fixing me up to look nice in my coffin, but he tied my shoes, buttoned my shirt and kept a tight lip, which was all right with me. I couldn't wear a coat so he loaned me a sweater that was too small even after he had opened up the left shoulder with a pair of scissors and pinned it together over the cast. It hurt him to cut up a good sweater on my account.

If don Ubaldo had told him anything about our conversation, he didn't show it. He helped me out to the street, where don Ubaldo's car waited. I was surprised to see that Julie was going along on the trip. She seemed puzzled herself. She could only be accompanying us on don Ubaldo's invitation, and he liked her about as much as he liked me. I guessed that the old man was putting her on trial as a possible gift to his son, the way he would try out a new horse before he bought it for Raul's birthday.

Ana Luz went along, too, and an officer of the Guardia Civil. The *comandante* was a slick pretty boy who wore the same kind of shiny boots that the mousy cop had worn who investigated Berrien's death aboard the *Talca*, but that was their only resemblance. The *comandante's* prettiness didn't hide the fact that he was as sharp as a tack. He shook my good hand, said he was honored to have my cooperation, and told me, during the first half hour of the drive, of the steps he had taken to bottle Jeff. From what he had to say, Jeff would have a tough time getting out of Peru, with or without the gold.

I gave him what information I could—a description of Tacho, a description of the clothes they had worn, the markings of the burros, nothing much that he didn't already know. And I said, "Has the news gone out that I am dead?"

"Your sad death has been reported to all the newspapers." He flashed his teeth. "Also to the wind, on which news travels faster. You hope that Jefferson will hear of it?"

"Yes. He told me once that he had smuggled things from Puno across the lake to Bolivia, where he had the connections he needed to dispose of them. If he thinks I am unable to interfere with him, he may try it again. We should catch him in Puno."

"If he has not already crossed the lake."

"I don't see how he could have got there yet. He has to drive three burros over two hundred miles through the hills, if the roads are guarded as strongly as you say. He might try another way across the border, but…"

"I doubt it. North of the lake there is nothing but high mountains, covered with snow at all times, and to pass the lake to the south would mean an extra hundred-mile journey. Besides, the borders are strongly guarded—except at Puno, as you suggested. Once he enters the town he is in a trap—so." The *comandante* cupped his hands and brought them together. "Anyone can enter the town. There are two hundred men on hand to prevent him from leaving it."

"You really mean business, don't you?"

"Don Ubaldo is an important man in Peru. If he says the hunt is in the national interest, we do as he asks."

Naharro said nothing. He was sitting in the front seat of the car, between Raul, who drove, and the *comandante*. I think he had taken the front seat so he would not have to look at me and Ana Luz, or talk to us. I rode in back, on the left side, where I could prop my cast up in the corner. Ana Luz sat next to me, so she could grab me when the car hit a rough spot, and Julie sat on her right. I wore a steel corset which supported the cast and made me sit up a lot straighter than normally, but Ana Luz's arms around me over the bumps helped a lot.

We were stopped half a dozen times by *guardias* who snapped to attention when they saw the *comandante*. Each time he asked if they had any news to report. The answer was always no. At La Raya, a dingy, chilly town on the crest of the Andean divide where we took time out for lunch, the *comandante* disappeared for fifteen minutes and came back with the report that everything was going according to plan. Jeff could move freely as long as he kept going toward Puno.

I had to translate the conversation for Julie. Raul didn't talk to her, and nobody else could, although the *comandante* tried his shiny teeth and a few words of English on her a couple of times. He would have liked to flirt a little with the *gringa* to pass time during the long drive, but she was on her best behavior, anxious to please Raul and the old man. The *comandante* gave up.

Raul didn't talk to anybody, except to answer yes or no when he was spoken to. Something was going on that he didn't know about, and he didn't like it. If there hadn't been any other tipoff, Ana Luz's appearance alone would have been enough. I never saw such a change in a woman. Before, she had been pretty enough, but lifeless, indifferent, rarely smiling, never laughing, going about her business without an unnecessary word. Now she glowed with life. She was like a lamp. The change showed in her eyes, her movements, her quick smile, everything. She was alive, for the first time.

During lunch, I caught don Ubaldo watching her with a strange, sad look. From her face, his eyes went to Raul's, then to Julie's. When he saw me looking at him, his swollen eyelids dropped. He went on eating.

I pulled my hat down over my forehead, crouching as low as the steel corset and the cast would let me, when we drove into Puno late that afternoon. It was the *comandante's* idea to keep me out of sight—probably an unnecessary caution, he said, but he liked to be careful. And I gave a false name at the Hotel Turismo. It had been five days since Jeff left Cuzco with the burros. A man with plenty of guts and no mercy for his animals might have covered the ground in that time. He wouldn't show up at the Hotel Turismo in any event, but the *comandante* had the right idea. It paid to be careful with a man like Jeff.

It was bitterly cold in Puno, even colder than it had been when we crossed the divide. We were at twelve thousand five hundred feet, on the lake shore, and the tremendous body of water that was Titicaca, the highest lake in the world, acted like a refrigerator. Even if the *comandante* hadn't told me to stay inside the hotel, I wouldn't have left the roaring fire in the *sala* once I settled there. The room was empty, except for me and the fire and a hot rum punch the barman brought me. The *comandante* had left to check his traps. Everybody else was warming up with a hot bath. I couldn't bathe, so I settled for the rum punch and the comfort of the fireplace.

I was sipping my drink when Ana Luz came into the *sala* and sat down beside me.

Conversation between us was difficult to start, as always. I finally said, "Would you like a rum punch?"

"No, thank you. Don Ubaldo doesn't like…"

She stopped. Her eyes widened. In a tone of complete surprise, she said, "Why, I can have a rum punch if I want to."

"*Claro.* Or anything else you want."

She hugged herself.

"I can't believe it. All my life—oh, I can't believe it! To be able to go where I like, do as I wish, answer to no one. If only they catch Jefferson! Do you really think they will catch him?"

"What difference does it make?"

"It was the bargain you made."

"I made no bargain with don Ubaldo, except to tell him what I knew in exchange for his promises."

She shook her head.

"The treasure will have to be recovered. Otherwise…"

"Otherwise nothing. He said you were free."

"No. I am not free—yet. Not truly free. But soon—I hope—I hope—oh, I'm afraid to think of it!"

She hugged herself again, wrapping her arms tightly across her breast as if she were embracing something precious. I sipped my rum punch, knowing I could never convince her that Jeff's capture was not part of the bargain. Don Ubaldo had cared as carefully for her mind as he had for her health.

Raul and Julie came into the *sala* together. Raul was sullen, Julie miserable. I was beginning to think that I might be doing her a dirty trick in turning Raul loose for her. When I asked them if they wanted a drink, he answered shortly that she'd have a hot lemonade and he'd have a rum punch—but he'd buy the round. It wasn't a friendly gesture. He just didn't want to be obligated to me. I said I didn't care who paid for it. Then don Ubaldo came in and made the same offer. I accepted again. With three hot drinks in me, I should have felt good.

But I didn't. I couldn't stop worrying about Jeff. He was smart. Would he walk into the trap? Or was he

beating it down to the seacoast right now, while we sat
around like dummies? I knew that everybody else in the
room was thinking the same thing. Don Ubaldo sat
down for a while, and then got up to pace nervously in
front of the fire, back and forth, back and forth. Ana
Luz watched the blaze, dreaming. Raul stared at his
glass. Julie looked from the fire to Raul to me to Ana
Luz to don Ubaldo and back along the same round,
alone and excluded and unhappy until Raul's hand—
they were sitting side by side—half-indifferently closed
over hers. And when I saw the expression that came
into her face, I thought, You little two-bit tin god,
damned if you haven't got something. I don't know what
it is, but…

There was a flash of light through the window, a
scream of brakes as a car roared to a halt outside the
hotel. Somebody yelled something I didn't catch,
except for my own name. Everybody jumped. The
comandante burst into the *sala*, his face red with cold,
his eyes blazing.

"We've found a body!" he shouted. "I think it's the
Indian, Tacho! It answers your description! Come
along!"

I jumped to my feet. Even at the moment, Ana Luz's
reaction was automatic. She said, "Wait! Your shoulder!
I'll get a blanket," and hurried away.

She tucked the blanket around my cast and shoulders after we had all piled into the car outside. Nobody
stayed behind. It was a big car, a station wagon, but
even then it was crowded, with a *guardia* driving and
another standing on the running board. We roared away

from the hotel, splashed up a muddy street, past the railroad station and down toward the lake, following a rutted track that led off across the flat barren shore toward the brightly lighted mole where the night boat for Bolivia waited, and then turned away to skirt the dark lake shore for half a mile to a patch of reeds growing at the water's edge.

Two *guardias* waited for us near the reed patch. One carried an oil lantern. The other held the wrist of a scared Indian, muffled to the eyes in *poncho* and *chullo*, a scarf around his neck and mouth to keep out the night air and his legs bare to the knees. His feet and ankles were covered with black mud.

The lantern light fell on a body lying face down in the mud. A hurried attempt had been made to bury it there. I saw the shallow hole scooped out among the reeds, and the red stain of blood floating on black water. The *poncho* that covered the body had a big blotch of blood under the left shoulder blade. When the *guardia* with the lantern lifted the body so I could see the face, a trickle of blood and *coca*-stained saliva drooled from the muddy mouth.

The *guardia* let the body fall at my nod.

"It's Tacho," I said. "How long has he been dead?"

"Not very long." The *comandante* was hot with excitement. "This Indian says the body was warm when he found it. He was stealing reeds to make a *balsa*—the lake reeds are dying out, and cutting them is prohibited—when he stumbled over it. He had to go see a priest before he could make up his mind to report it, so we lost about an hour. But he can't have been dead more than two or three hours, at the most. Jefferson is in Puno now! We've got him!"

Behind me, Ana Luz drew a long breath.

I said, "I hope so. But you had better tip off the guard to be on the alert."

"I've already done it. Their instructions are to shoot anybody who doesn't stop at a challenge. We've caught him now! He can't go back the way he came, and if he tries to take the boat to Bolivia he's finished."

"I hope so. Didn't anybody hear the shot?"

"There wasn't any shot. He was knifed—in the back. Your friend Jefferson is going to hang."

One of the *guardias* took the Indian, scared dumb, off to the town lockup on a charge of cutting reeds—a big patch had been slashed out of the middle of the clump near Tacho's body—and the other *guardia* stayed behind with the lantern to watch the body until it could be removed. Raul took Ana Luz and Julie back to the hotel in the station wagon. The *comandante*, don Ubaldo and I walked along the lake shore to the mole where the steamer was getting ready to shove off for Guaqui, on the Bolivian side.

It didn't leave on time, that night. A sergeant with a squad of men was in charge of the mooring lines when we got there, paying no attention to the complaints he was getting from passengers, crew and captain. The *comandante* split the squad into couples and sent them over the ship.

She was pretty big for a ship that must have come up from sea level in pieces, certainly big enough to hide a stowaway. I went along with the *comandante* to watch the search. The job took about an hour, including the time we spent listening to the captain, a *boliviano*, grumble about his sailing time while he trailed us around and did his best to get in our way without making it too obvious that he hoped we wouldn't find whatever we were looking for. But the search was a good one. We drew a blank. The surly captain got his clearance, lines were cast off, the steamer chugged away into the dark. The *comandante* and I went back to where don Ubaldo waited on the mole.

"That's all we can do tonight," the *comandante* said. "The town is sealed tight. In the morning we'll start a house-to-house search."

"When does the next boat leave?" don Ubaldo asked.

"A freight vessel sails in the morning. I am posting a guard to check every man and every bit of cargo that goes aboard her."

I said, "Suppose he gets by you, somehow, and reaches the Bolivian side. Can't you bring him back on a murder charge?"

The *comandante* shrugged.

"Legally, yes. Actually, they do not like us in Bolivia. They still blame Peru because we were unable to prevent Chile from stealing their coastal provinces during the War of the Pacific. And their police would not have the same interest we have. With the treasure he is carrying, he would have little difficulty in buying his way free. But I assure you that he will never escape Peru now. I suggest that you both go back to the hotel and get some sleep. I will call for you in the morning."

He left us to give orders to the sergeant.

Don Ubaldo and I walked back from the mole to the hotel, without a word to say to each other. It wasn't more than a quarter of a mile, but my legs were shaky before I got there. The cast and the steel corset were heavy under my blanket.

Raul, Ana Luz and Julie were waiting in the *sala*. I said, "Nothing," and flopped down in a chair, worn out.

Julie said, "Who was the—dead man?"

"An Indian who helped us dig up the gold."

"Why did he kill him?"

"I don't know. Unloading excess baggage, I guess, the way he tried to do with me. One man has a better chance to get away than two."

Julie shuddered.

"He seemed so—ordinary, on the ship. I never thought…"

She didn't finish it. We sat around, looking at the fire for another half hour, and then I had to move or pass out in my chair. I got up and said I was going to bed.

"I'll help you take your clothes off," Raul said.

He hadn't ever thought of anybody else in his life. I knew he wasn't thinking of my comfort now. He wanted to talk about something. In my room, I let him help me with buttons and shoelaces until he got around to what was bothering him.

"What's going on?" he said abruptly.

I was brushing my teeth. He sat on the edge of the bathtub, watching me. I said, "What's going on with who?"

"Ana Luz. My father. Me. You. Julie. All of us."

"You haven't talked to your old man?"

"I don't have to talk to him to know that something is happening. What's it all about?"

I rinsed off the toothbrush and hung it on a hook.

"I've been reshuffling the deck a little," I said. "An ace and a deuce don't go well together. You're the deuce. Ana Luz is the ace."

"What do you mean?"

"I mean I bought Ana Luz from you and your father, that's all. She isn't going to marry you."

He nodded craftily.

"I knew you wanted her, ever since that night on the ship. You weren't in her cabin just because you knew she had been in yours. You thought you had something to trade with. But she was too much for you, wasn't she? I saw those marks over your eyes, even if nobody else did. You…"

I still had a good punch left in my right hand. I let him have it. He fell over into the bathtub and cracked his head against the wall. His eyes went out of focus for a couple of seconds. When they steadied again—he was balanced on his shoulders, his feet up in the air—I said, "I can lick you with one hand, *guagua*. I'd just as soon do it now as any other time. Get up."

He crawled out of the bathtub. I took another crack at him. He ducked under it and slid through the bathroom door. I had to go sideways through the door, because of the cast, and he got away before I could catch him.

But one punch was better than none, and I had been saving it up for him for a long time.

17

I cooled down while I was dabbing iodine on my knuckles. There was no heat in the rooms, but when I crawled into bed I found that somebody had put a hot-water bottle between the sheets. I wondered if it was Ana Luz or the hotel management. Probably Ana Luz. She really was an ace, that girl. If I never accomplished anything else, I had done something to free her from Raul. *If* I had freed her. She'd never feel free in her own mind unless we caught Jeff and recovered the treasure. But we had to catch him now. He was trapped. Or was he? I wasn't as sure of it as the *comandante* was. And if he did give us the slip, get away to Bolivia somehow, everything I had done had been a waste of time. I would have spent five or six hundred dollars of my own money and three weeks of my time for nothing. The money and the time didn't amount to much. The important things were what I had promised Ana Luz, and hoped to do for Julie. Playing God isn't a good thing if you can't deliver. I remembered Julie's face when Raul had held her hand, and Ana Luz's face as she hugged herself in front of the fire, afraid to think of what might be hers because it wasn't hers yet. Lying there in the dark, so tired I couldn't sleep, I saw Naharro's face as it had been when he told me how much the recovery of the treasure meant to him; Jeff's face, with the wolf grin, looking at me over the pistol, the hammer going back; Tacho's face, empty and ugly, blood and saliva trickling from his mouth; Berrien's face, calm and peaceful in death. Dead man, live men, thieves, liars, murderers, cheats, their lives tied to three hundred pounds of metal and polished stones.

The sleep I got that night was only an occasional doze. My mind wouldn't stop going around in the squirrel cage. I couldn't find a comfortable position in the steel corset, and when I did drop off, the altitude brought me awake gasping for breath, so that I had to sit up and take deep gulps of air. My shoulder itched inside the cast. I wanted a cigarette, didn't have any within reach, and was too cold to get out of bed and look for them. I wanted a drink. I wanted it to be morning, so the search could start. I wanted to get it over with, one way or another. I wanted to get out of Puno, get out of Peru, go somewhere, anywhere...

The dawn came at last. When it was light enough to see, I got up, shivered clumsily into my clothes, and wrapped a blanket around my shoulders. Frost was thick on the thatched roofs of the mud huts under the hotel window, and glistened whitely on the sparse grass of the flat sloping down to the lake shore. Lights were still on at the mole, where another steamer had tied up during the night.

I left the hotel quietly and walked down to the mole, frozen mud and grass crackling under my feet. The *comandante* was already on the job, giving instructions to the sergeant and his squad of soldiers. They all looked cold and tired. The lake was like glass, without the faintest swell to rock the steamer tied up at the mole—the steamer that was Jeff's only chance of escape. The hunt had begun.

"It may take some time," the *comandante* said. "There are a couple of thousand houses. But I have men working in toward the center of town from all sides, and he can't skip around like a flea with three hundred pounds of gold. We'll find him before long."

"When does the steamer leave?"

"As soon as she's loaded. My men were on hand when she tied up. They're checking everything that goes on her. Let's go aboard and have coffee."

We had coffee in the *salón*. It was served, grudgingly, by a *mozo* who didn't like Peruvians or *gringos,* a *boliviano* from the way he scowled at the *comandante's* uniform. The *comandante* got a lot of scowls. The ship's captain wasn't around to grumble at us, but most of the crew were *bolivianos,* still fighting the War of the Pacific. It was easy to see that they weren't on our side, even if they didn't know what the excitement was all about.

We finished our coffee and went back to the mole. Loading was slow, because of the inspection. The sergeant was already getting complaints that the ship wouldn't make her sailing time. He went stolidly on with his job.

The *comandante* said, "There's nothing for us to do here. I want to see how the search is going. Come along."

He had the station wagon waiting. We drove up toward town until we met the first batch of *guardias* working their way in toward the central plaza, house by house.

Except for the hotel, the railroad station, and a few big buildings in the center of town, Puno is mostly mud and thatch, one- or two-room huts. Two *guardias* went into each hut, their rifles ready, while the rest of a squad waited outside. There would be a cackle of Indian indignation from inside the hut, and then the two *guardias* would come out, join their companions, and fan out to pass the hut on both sides, moving on to the next house or stable or chicken hutch, whatever lay in their way. The *comandante* and I trailed along.

The sun came up across the lake, red and gold through the cold mist rising from the water. Fishing *balsas,* clumsy-looking reed boats, some with straw sails, began to put out from the shore. The town lay in the bight of an inlet, low headlands stretching out into the lake on either side, and the fishermen in the *balsas* paddled slowly for the mouth of the inlet, out toward the deep water of the lake where fish were to be caught.

I said to the *comandante,* "Is somebody checking those *balsas* out?"

"Of course."

The sun rose higher. The search went on, hut by hut, street by street. I saw soldiers helping the *guardias.* The soldiers were all young kids, conscripts in shabby brown uniforms from the town *cuartel,* having a whale of a time doing something besides drill. One of them must have had an itchy trigger finger, because we heard a shot down the street and ran to investigate. It was a false alarm, a baby wailing in fright, its mother yelling curses, nobody hurt. We followed along as the ring grew smaller, closing in on the plaza like a clenched fist.

The steamer hooted from the mole, a series of short, impatient blasts on her whistle. The *comandante* looked at his watch. A messenger on a burro came trotting down the street, pulled up in front of the *comandante,* saluted without getting out of his saddle, and said, "The steamer is ready to leave, señor *comandante.* Is it permitted?"

"Everything has been checked?"

"Everything. The *sargento* reports all in order."

The *comandante* bit his thumbnail. The steamer hooted again, as impatiently as before. The *comandante* said, "Very well. Tell the *sargento* to leave two men at the mole and bring the rest of the squad here—after the steamer has sailed."

The man on the burro saluted, wheeled his animal, kicked with his heels, and trotted away.

The *comandante* bit his thumbnail again. We followed along behind the searchers.

"I'm nervous," the *comandante* said frankly, minutes later. "I don't like this. We're getting too near the center of town."

"No chance that he's slipped aboard the ship?"

"None. That's a good sergeant."

"How about the railroad?"

"The station is under guard. Everything is under guard. *Carajo,* he must be moving along ahead of us. But with all that weight…"

The steamer's whistle interrupted him with two final triumphant hoots. Her lines were in. She was ready to sail.

"Those *balsas*…"

I had turned to look at the lake, where the fishing

boats were still paddling slowly for the mouth of the inlet, their sails useless in the morning calm. The *comandante* turned with me, a frown on his face. But he shook his head positively.

"Every man in them had to show his papers to my men. And it's thirty-five miles across the lake to the nearest point. Even an Indian wouldn't try it in a *balsa*."

"Jeff isn't an Indian."

The *comandante* shook his head again.

"It's impossible. He's here, somewhere."

He turned back to follow the *guardias,* who had moved ahead two huts while we were talking.

I watched the steamer back away from the mole, turn in a tight circle, and pick up speed toward the mouth of the inlet. She was fast. She would reach the open lake before the *balsas* did. The men in the *balsas* knew it, too, because when she hooted her whistle I saw them stop paddling and gesture warningly at each other. The *comandante's* men had delayed them a few minutes too long. They couldn't get through the mouth of the inlet before the steamer caught up with them, and if she passed them in the narrow channel her wash would swamp them. They separated like a flock of scared ducks, paddling away toward the shore on either side to give the steamer a free passage.

And that beat Jeff. Because when the steamer cleared the mouth of the inlet and nosed out into the lake, there was no protective screen of fishing boats near her to hide the single *balsa* that put out from the headland, the man in it paddling hard to head the steamer off. He must have been desperate when the fishing boats that would have covered his escape turned back at the last minute. But it was his chance. He took it, gambling to the last, rather than wait there on the bare headland, anchored to his loot, to be hunted down like a rabbit when the *guardias* finished searching the town and fanned out to beat the countryside.

I bellowed at the *comandante,* half a block up the street. I was already running back toward the station wagon when he caught up with me.

"What is it?" he yelled.

"Jeff. Hurry." Running was difficult, with the heavy cast to throw me off balance at each step. I needed my wind.

"Where?"

"*Balsa.* Off the headland."

He looked over his shoulder as he ran, saw the small boat paddling furiously to cut the steamer off, and asked no more questions. He reached the station wagon ahead of me and had the motor going when I jumped in. We roared away toward the mole, the horn going steadily, Indians, burros and llamas jumping for their lives ahead of us.

I said, "Is there a launch?"

"Yes. We'll get him. Where did he come from?"

"The headland. That Indian you put in jail didn't cut those reeds. Jeff and Tacho did. Jeff turned his burros loose, killed Tacho because he didn't need him any more, lugged the reeds out to the headland before Tacho's body was discovered, and spent the night tying a *balsa* together. Can you catch the steamer?"

"If it slows down to pick him up."

"Will they be fools enough to try it?"

"Probably. Those *bolivianos* would enjoy thumbing their noses at us, and they can make Bolivian waters before we could do anything about it. But they can't take him aboard without cutting speed. We'll get him."

The station wagon skidded on wet rails as we hit the spur track leading from the railroad yard to the mole. It slewed around, its wheels spinning, and bogged down in mud. We jumped out and ran the last few yards.

The two *guardias* the sergeant had left on guard were loafing on a bench. They jumped up, grabbing their rifles, when they saw the *comandante* running toward them. He shouted and waved toward the ladder that led down to the water's edge, halfway between us and them.

They got it. They were ahead of us when we ran down the ladder to a float where half a dozen small boats were tied up. A *cholo* was slapping white lead on the hull of one of the boats, a launch with a gasoline kicker. He had careened it against the float with a couple of lines so he could paint below the water line.

The two *guardias* were casting off his lines before he knew what was happening. He opened his mouth to yell, but the *comandante* shut him up.

"Catch the steamer! Hurry!"

The *cholo* knew authority when he heard it. He dropped his paint brush and jumped for the kicker. We piled in. The *comandante* picked up an oar from the bottom of the boat, pushed away from the float, and then, because the engine didn't catch right away, began to paddle uselessly. The engine coughed, roared, coughed again, and began to hum. The *cholo* put the wheel hard over.

The steamer whistled. Her pilot had spotted the man in the *balsa,* crazily wig-wagging his arms. Jeff had given up paddling, seeing that he couldn't make it, and was staking everything on his signals and, I suppose, shouted promises of a fortune for every man aboard. He must have felt hell's own fury in his heart when the steamer did slow down at his shouts and arm-waving, and he saw us skipping across the water toward him, the *guardias'* rifles glinting in the sun, the *comandante* erect in the bow of the launch, a revolver in his hand.

Jeff's nerve never failed him, even then. He would have reached the side of the ship before us if the wash from her backed engines hadn't pushed his *balsa* away. Somebody threw him a line that fell short. Before the line could be hauled in and tossed again, the launch had swooped in around the stern of the steamer. The *cholo* boatman cut his motor. The roar of the kicker faded. The launch rolled as it came about between the steamer and the *balsa*.

In the sudden quiet, I said, "Hello, Jeff."

Five yards separated us. Both boats rocked in the wash, slowly coming together as the launch's kicker ticked over. The *guardias* waited, their rifles ready. The *comandante* covered Jeff with his revolver. Heads lined the rail of the steamer above us.

All Jeff saw was me, the cast holding my arm up by my ear in what must have looked to him like a mocking greeting from the grave, the end of everything for him.

His dirty face, scrubby in a week's growth of beard, twisted. He reached under his *poncho*.

The *comandante let* him get the gun out before his own gun slammed in my ear. The *guardias'* rifles banged a split second later. All three bullets hit Jeff in the chest. His reflexes shocked him to his feet, but he must have been dead before he crumpled and fell. The rickety *balsa* tipped as his body hit the gunwale. It rocked once, shipped water, and went down like a stone.

18

The diver that Naharro called up from Callao to get the gold from the lake bottom had no trouble finding it. It had gone straight down with the *balsa,* and the water wasn't deep off the mouth of the inlet. The diver's only difficulty was with his air-compression apparatus, which didn't work right at such a high altitude. He wasn't used to the cold water, either. But he found all ninety-three pieces.

Jeff's body floated up on the shore and was buried there in Puno, next to Tacho's grave. I didn't see the burial or watch the diver working, because I was in bed for four days after I passed out as I was leaving the launch at the mole. It was only fatigue and general weakness that bothered me, but I took it easy for a while and let Ana Luz wait on me. She and I were alone in Puno after Naharro and the *comandante* went to

Lima with the treasure and Raul took Julie back to Arequipa. Ana Luz used to spend hours at my bedside, reading to me or playing cards with me or just dreaming, a glow in her face.

Once she said, "Is it difficult to learn English?"

"No more difficult than learning any other language, except for the spelling. Why do you want to learn English?"

"I want to go to the States. I want to live in New York, get a job there, go to theatres and lectures and concerts every night, live like a North American. Do you know, I've never been out of Peru except for that one trip to Chile with don Alfredo. I was never farther from Arequipa than Lima until I became his nurse."

"It's expensive, living in New York. Not like here."

"I have some money. I saved all the salary that don Alfredo paid me. And I should be able to get some kind of a job nursing in a big city like New York. Is it as big as they say?"

"The biggest city in the world. The biggest, noisiest and most exciting, if you have never been there."

She sighed, her eyes bright.

"When are you going to leave?"

"As soon as you are well."

"I'm well now. Don't let me hold you."

"I owe you too much to leave now. I can never repay you, but…"

"Stop it."

"No. I can never forget it. I swear I will not, as long as I live."

"Foolishness. Let's play cards."

I got up on the fifth day. A letter from don Ubaldo and a telegram from the *comandante* arrived at the same time. The *comandante* was in trouble for killing Jeff. The United States Embassy didn't like the idea of Peruvian police shooting United States nationals, whatever they happened to be doing, and the *comandante* needed my story to help square him. That was enough reason to take me to Lima, because he was a good guy and I liked him. Another reason was Naharro's letter. The National Institute of Archaeology, he wrote, wanted me to attend a dinner they were having in my honor, at which the discovery of the treasure would be announced and the discovery reward paid.

The letter was about as warm as the third one you get from a bill collector after you have ignored the first two. He didn't ask after my health, and he didn't ask after Ana Luz.

So I took her to Lima with me. She had to go there anyway, to get a visa for the United States, and she said there was no reason for her to return to Arequipa. She never wanted to see Arequipa again. All she wanted to take with her was the clothes she wore. I think she would have sent those back if she could have bought others in Puno, stripped her body bare of everything connected with her old life as she had stripped her mind of its obligation when the treasure at last rose from the lake.

We took the train back to Cuzco. I found my bag in Tacho's hut, just as I had left it. His woman was there. I told her that Tacho was dead and gave her some money. She took it without a word or a change of expression. She was nursing her dirty baby when I left the hut.

In Cuzco we caught a plane that put us down in Lima the next day. I looked up the *comandante* first, told him to stop worrying, and then went on to the Embassy to give them as much of the story as was necessary to get them to drop out of the picture. Afterwards I hunted up a doctor and had him knock the cast off my shoulder and fix a black satin sling for my arm. I didn't need the sling, but the banquet was set for that night. I wanted to look properly battered when I stood up to accept the reward for all my trouble on behalf of the Republic of Peru.

It was quite a banquet. The *Instituto Nacional de Arqueología* took over most of the Hotel Bolívar, where I had first opened Berrien's package and seen the manuscript. Ana Luz went to the banquet with me, in a new evening dress that was so nearly of the same material as my satin arm sling that they could have been cut from the same bolt of cloth. I looked real distinguished, with the sling on one arm and her on the other. The *comandante* was there, all clear since I had talked to the Embassy. Raul was there with Julie. He stayed far enough away from me so I couldn't have hit him even if I had felt like it, but Julie waved hello. I didn't have a chance to ask her how she was getting along before Naharro saw me.

His face froze when I walked in with Ana Luz. But he had to make the introductions, whether he liked it or not, and he carried them off as if he weren't wishing that we would both drop dead. There were about a hundred and fifty old badgers and their wives who wanted to meet the *gringo* hero, so dinner was served before I had finished going the rounds.

The speeches began while the last plates were being cleared away. The president of the Institute was toastmaster. He couldn't wait to get started. He stood up, banged a wine glass with his knife for attention, and let go with a flood of oratory.

"*Socios del Instituto, señoras y convidados distinguidos.* It is my privilege this evening to introduce our guest of honor, a *norteamericano* whose name will go down in Peruvian history along with the names of Francisco Pizarro, José de San Martín, Simón Bolívar and others who have contributed to the progress of our fair country. Before presenting our distinguished guest, it was my intention to make formal announcement of the discovery of a truly amazing collection of Incaic treasure which the Institute is now preparing for public exhibition. However—" he giggled happily "—since the discovery has been the sole subject of conversation of everyone present for several days, the announcement seems unnecessary. I will only say that we expect the Treasure of Amarú to be recognized by the world of archaeology as one of the most significant finds ever made in Peru. I will have more to say about it later. In the meantime, I am sure that you are all less interested in listening to my own poor words than to the story of the discovery of the treasure from the lips of the discoverer himself. *Señoras y señores*, I give you—Señor Al Colby!"

The applause roared. Ana Luz smiled encouragingly as I stood up, cleared my throat, and stalled with a drink of water.

The toastmaster had thrown me a hot potato. I hadn't expected to have to say any more than "Thanks."

I didn't know how much of the truth Naharro had told him, and I could put my foot in it good if I talked too much.

I said, "*Señoras y señores,* your distinguished president embarrasses me with praise. My own small part in the discovery was possible only because I was fortunate enough to come into possession of a portion of a manuscript which led me to the treasure. Without the kind assistance of don Ubaldo Naharro, your associate, who obtained for me a permit to carry out the search, and the help of your justly famous *Guardia Civil* under the leadership of the *comandante* sitting opposite me—" I had forgotten his name and he knew it, but he grinned and nodded. "—I would never have been here this evening. The unearthing of the treasure was simply a matter of following instructions in the manuscript which I have mentioned. I believe that Señor Naharro knows as much of the history of this interesting document as any man living. I suggest that you call on him for a few words. *Gracias.*"

I sat down, sweating. The hot potato was Naharro's now. Damn it, where was my check? I wasn't there just for a speech of welcome. If he had double-crossed me at the last minute...

Naharro stood up as the applause died. He didn't look in my direction.

"What Señor Colby says is true," he began slowly. "I think I know as much as any man alive of the manuscript to which he refers. You have all heard the story of the message of the last Villac Umu, the key to an enormous treasure which was hidden from the *con-*

207

quistadores by the Inca priests. You probably thought, as I did at one time, that it was only another legend. It is not a legend. The manuscript which—came into Señor Colby's possession consisted of three pieces of parchment containing instructions leading to what our president has referred to as the Treasure of Amarú, a magnificent discovery. While those pieces of parchment have served their purpose and no longer have material value, they would have made an interesting addition to the Institute's collection. I regret to say that they have been accidentally destroyed."

I was reaching for my water glass when he said that. I almost knocked it over. When I looked up, he was waiting, his face still turned toward his audience, as if thinking over what he would say next. I knew that he was waiting for me.

I could have called him a liar then and there, I suppose. But I still didn't have my check, I could still land in trouble any time he wanted to put me there, and I still didn't know what he was up to. If he wanted to keep the three pieces of parchment, we both knew that I wasn't in any position to argue about it. But I was puzzled.

He gave me plenty of time before he went on.

"The regrettable thing is not the destruction of this portion of the manuscript, since the treasure to which it was the key has been unearthed. The tragedy is that the rest of the manuscript, which might well have led to archaeological wealth beside which the Treasure of Amarú would represent only an insignificant collection of toys, has been irretrievably lost to the world. There were nine other pieces of parchment, originally. What message they bore can only be conjectured. But we all know the immense value of the objects hidden during the last days of Cuzco, when the *conquistadores* swept up the Road of Kings from Cajamarca...."

I wasn't listening to him. I knew what he was doing, now.

The message on the three sheets of parchment didn't have to be conjectured. They said enough to prove that the legend of the fourteen gold statues under the middle wall of the fortress of Sacsahuamán was true. If the Institute ever got hold of that part of the manuscript, they wouldn't need instructions how to get to the hidden chamber. They would take the fortress wall apart stone by stone. Naharro wasn't going to have that. Let them gloat over the Treasure of Amarú. He would keep his secret until a time came when it was safe for him to dig. Only Al Colby could tip over his applecart, and if Al Colby knew on which side his bread was buttered, he'd keep his mouth shut. If not...

A spatter of applause drowned the end of Naharro's speech. He bowed and sat down. The toastmaster bobbed to his feet.

"And now, *señoras y señores, I* have only a few more words to say." His mind was so full of something else that he hadn't noticed that neither Naharro nor I had said a single word about the discovery of the parchment, where, when or how. "First, it is my pleasure to present to Señor Colby this small token of appreciation from the Republic of Peru for his truly remarkable contribution to our archaeology—a check for seven hundred and fifty thousand *soles de oro!*"

An excited buzz ran around the table. I swallowed hard as I took the check. Seven hundred and fifty thousand *soles* was fifty thousand dollars in hard money. I couldn't think of a thing to say except *"Muchísimas gracias."* The toastmaster barely let me get that much out.

"A large reward, you will say. But well earned, as you may judge for yourself." His voice rose and cracked. He clapped his hands loudly. "Behold—the Treasure of Amarú!"

Double doors at the end of the dining room swung open. Heads turned. There was a startled silence, a gasp, and then a scramble.

It was a private showing among friends, so only six cops were on hand, with ropes strung to keep the crowd from getting too close to the tables on which the collection stood under floodlights. You can see it today in the Inca Museum, although you have to get special permission to look at it. It was beautiful stuff after they finished polishing it. Not all of it was polished then, but enough had been done to make a lot of archaeological mouths water. One sun-disk, cleaned and burnished like a mirror, must have weighed thirty pounds, solid hammered gold. The corn-plant statues were the finest workmanship, perfect reproductions of the stalk and leaves in gold, the ear and its tassel in silver sheathed with a gold husk, less than two feet high overall but complete in every detail, as finely made as a fine watch. Other pieces were studded with emeralds as big as your thumbnail. Some of the animal statuettes had jade eyeballs set in silver, others were just chunks of solid, soft gold.

I thought of the golden vicuña, and counted the

pieces. There were ninety-four. It must have wrenched Naharro to give up that last piece, but he had compensated himself for it, in a way, because a printed card on one of the tables read:

The Treasure of Amarú
Discovered in Cuzco Province by Al Colby and
Ubaldo Naharro, I.N.A.
April, 1948

I was reading the card when Julie came over to where Ana Luz and I were pressed up against the ropes. I had never liked her so much as I did when she held out her hand to Ana Luz and said, in clumsy Spanish, "I am glad for you. I heard that you—obtained—what you wish for. I hope you will be very happy."

Ana Luz said, *"Gracias,"* and meant it.

"Glad for me, too?" I showed Julie the check.

"Oh, yes. I'm glad for everyone."

She didn't look it. Her smile was mechanical. I said, "How are you getting along with Raul?"

"All right."

"You don't seem very happy about it."

"It's not Raul. It's don Ubaldo. He still thinks I'm a tramp." She sighed unhappily. "I've tried everything. I've been so damn ladylike that it hurts. I've even given up smoking because he doesn't approve of it. I just can't get anywhere with him."

"Why not run off with Raul, if you really want him? Let the old man soak in his own juice. You've got enough money for two, haven't you?"

"It isn't money. Raul won't do anything without his

father's approval. He's been under don Ubaldo's thumb all his life, just like…"

She stopped, looking sideways at Ana Luz. I said, "She doesn't understand English. You couldn't hurt her feelings anyway."

"…just like she was. That's what makes Raul the way he is—or the way he seems to be most of the time, sullen and disagreeable. He isn't, really. Underneath, he's sweet and nice, when I get him away from his father. He'll be wonderful as soon as don Ubaldo goes to Chile, but I still can't…"

"When is don Ubaldo going to Chile?"

"Tomorrow or the next day."

"What for?"

"I don't know. Business, I guess."

"How long is he going to be away?"

"I don't know."

My mind began to tick again.

There was more to it than I had thought. Fourteen gold statues weren't going to satisfy Naharro. He wanted everything. He didn't believe the other nine sheets of parchment were irretrievably lost, any more than I did. His speech had been a smokescreen, as much for my benefit as for the Institute's. He must have got hold of the name of the *hacendado* who wrote the letter to the museum, and now he was leaving for Chile. I didn't think it was a coincidence that the *hacendado* was *chileno*.

I turned to Ana Luz.

"What was the name of the *hacendado* who sold the parchment to Berrien?"

"I don't know."

"Weren't you there?"

"We met in the park, as you and don Alfredo did, and he was careful not to mention names. You know how cautious he was, even with me, whom he trusted—unwisely."

"The *hacendado* was of Santiago?"

"I don't think so. He must have come from out of town. We waited two days for him to keep the appointment."

"Where did he stay in Santiago?"

"I don't know."

"*Caramba,* you must know something about him. Would you recognize him if you saw him again?"

"Surely. He was very ugly. One of the ugliest men I ever saw."

I thought fast. I might be able to get the name from the museum, but it would take time—time I couldn't afford to waste if I was going to beat Naharro. And I was too much in the public eye just then to be able to ask questions at the museum without somebody wondering what it was all about.

I said, "Ana Luz, is the Chilean visa on your passport still good?"

"I think so. It was for three months."

"Will you do me one favor before you leave South America?"

She said simply, "You do not have to ask that question."

"Come back to Chile with me and help me find the *hacendado*."

"When?"

"Now. Tonight, if we can get a plane."

"I will have to pack a bag and change clothes."

"Go do it now. I'll meet you in the lobby in half an hour."

She turned away without a word and pushed through the crowd.

All this time Julie had stood there looking puzzled. She had not been able to follow the conversation, but she could tell that I was stirred up about something. I said, "You really want Raul, Julie? You're sure he's the man for you?"

"I'm sure—if I can get him away from his father."

"Then hang on to the leash until you hear from me. I may be able to buy him for you!"

The crowd was still too interested in the Treasure of Amarú to notice the guest of honor sneaking away early.

19

The breaks were with me that night. My papers were in order, I still had enough dollars left to pay for the tickets, and the DC 6, the big sleeper-plane, left for Santiago at midnight. It was half empty. I let the ticket clerk see the sling on my arm while I booked passage for Al Colby, North American, tourist, and Ana Luz Benavides, *Peruana*, nurse.

I took the sling off after the plane had left Limatambo airport and was snoring south through the night. I needed both hands, because Ana Luz couldn't draw. I sketched the outline of a head and spent an hour fitting in a dozen different noses over a dozen different mouths until I got a face that she said resembled the *hacendado*—perhaps the hairline a little lower here, the eyebrows heavier. When I had finished lowering the hairline and thickening the eyebrows, I had something ugly enough to satisfy her.

"It's recognizable," she said. "How will you use it?"

"Try all the hotels, first. Afterward, the banks. Berrien paid him five thousand dollars, American, for the parchment. That many dollars should have left a mark somewhere."

"And if you find him?"

"Trace the manuscript back until I find it or know that it's really lost."

"The treasure means so much to you, then?"

"The reward for its discovery does. And I would like to beat don Ubaldo. He leaves for Chile tomorrow or the next day."

"Why do you dislike don Ubaldo so much?"

I stared at her. She said, "He is not a bad man, only selfish. He would give his life to find the manuscript. Why do you not let him have it? You have already made enough money to satisfy an ordinary man."

"There is more to be made the same way. And I will turn anything I find over to the Republic, not keep it for my own enjoyment, as he would. He has no thought of sharing anything. He wants to own it, as he owned you."

"You do not know him. He would not have kept the treasure. He wanted the glory of finding it, yes. The thing that hurt him most was to see your name before his on the card that announced the discovery."

"There would have been no announcement if he had found it."

She said again, "You do not know him. He is not a miser, to surround himself with gold for his secret pleasure. He wants his name to be known to the world as that of a great archaeologist."

"So do I, then." She was beginning to irritate me. I couldn't understand her standing up for the old robber. I said, "You'd better get some sleep. We'll have plenty to do tomorrow."

"Very well. Good night."

"Good night."

The sleeper got into Santiago at nine-fifteen. Half an hour later we had cleared through customs and were working the hotels with my sketch. We tried the best ones first, then the second-class joints, then the scratch-houses. Ana Luz knew the date he had been in town, so it was only a matter of laying down the picture with a few *pesos* and asking a question. But nobody recognized the ugly face. If he had put up at one of a hundred *pensiones* or at a private house, the search was hopeless from that angle.

We tried the banks after lunch. I had had an account with the Bank of London and South America before leaving Santiago. I re-opened the account and asked the manager to collect my seven hundred and fifty thousand *soles* in dollars.

He laughed.

"It will take a month. You couldn't find that many dollars for sale in one piece on the whole West Coast.

Some days we don't pick up a hundred dollars worth of exchange in all of Santiago."

"Suppose I wanted to trace five thousand dollars that might have been sold here about a month ago. How would I go about it?"

"Check or cash?"

I asked Ana Luz. She said, "Cash."

The manager looked doubtful, but he rang a bell and sent his secretary to bring a big loose-leaf book showing daily exchange figures for all the banks in Santiago. While he was riffling the pages, he said, "The exchange is controlled, of course, but currency needn't have gone through a bank. If it was a private sale, there's no way to trace it. What was the date?"

"Just about thirty days ago. Not longer, maybe a few days less."

"On the fifth—that's thirty days—National City bought fifty-three hundred. Nothing big on the sixth. Nothing big on the seventh. On the eighth, we bought seven thousand. On the ninth, National City bought nearly nine thousand, Banco de Chile bought sixty-five hundred. On the tenth, nothing over five thousand. Of course, if it was sold in pieces, these figures don't mean anything either. The eleventh was Sunday. On the twelfth—"

"Wait a minute. I want to write those down."

After I got the figures, it was just footwork and good luck that we happened to talk to the clerk who had done business with our man. It was at the Banco de Chile, or we might not have learned anything even then. American and English banks are tougher about giving out information, as I knew from experience. But the clerk was young enough to be impressed by Ana Luz's good looks. When she showed him the sketch—I was counting on her to get farther with bank clerks than I could—he didn't shake his head as the others had done. He just looked doubtful.

"The nose is not quite right," Ana Luz said. "He is uglier even than the picture. He had five thousand dollars to sell, about a month ago."

"What is your interest in him, señorita?"

"Señora." She didn't blink an eye. "He is my husband."

I winced. We didn't know enough about him to take a chance like that. The clerk winced with me, but it was only the beauty-and-the-beast angle that hurt him. He said, "What is it that you wish to know?"

"The name he is using now, and where he lives. I must find him. Our child—our only child…"

She put her handkerchief to her mouth.

It was pretty crude, but it worked. The clerk asked a few more questions, weakening all the time. Ana Luz gave him some kind of a story about being deserted with a small child and no money. I didn't hear all she said, because I had my shoulders hunched up around my ears, waiting for the clerk to call a guard and have us thrown out in the street. But he fell for it. Our man wasn't a regular customer he had to protect, and the Chilean law helped us. Sellers of foreign exchange had to give their names and addresses to the buyers. The clerk looked the name up in his records, wrote on a slip of paper, and handed the paper to Ana Luz with a tear of sympathy in his eye.

She gave me the paper when we were out in the street. The name was Enrique Martínez Castro. The address was a post-office box number in Linares, a small farming town in the south.

Up until that minute, I hadn't thought about saying good-bye. We had been together so long, gone through so much together, that it seemed natural to have her with me. Seeing the address like that made me realize that she would be going one way and I another. But I didn't know how to make the break. She had never been easy to talk to, even when we had nothing final to say to each other. I suppose she felt the same way I did. We walked, silently, until we reached the river, turned east, and finally came to the *Parque Forestal*.

I was too busy thinking to notice where we were going. Ana Luz stopped me with her hand on my arm.

"Do you recognize this place?"

I looked around. The view of the river was familiar. So was the path, and the bench at its edge.

I said, "This is where I first talked to Berrien."

"Yes. Let's sit down for a minute."

"I'm sorry if I tired you. I was thinking."

"I'm not tired. But let's sit down."

We sat. She folded her hands, just as she had done the first day, and looked off at the river. It was a long time before she spoke.

"When are you going to Linares?"

"Tonight, if I can arrange it. I have to get there before Naharro does."

"You are still determined to beat him?"

"Nothing has happened to change my mind."

"You do not change your mind easily."

"No."

She said slowly, "I would do anything to change your mind about this thing."

"Why? What do you owe Naharro?"

"Nothing. You paid my debt. But I lived in his household for twenty years, grew up in it, looked on him as a father. He was kind to me, whatever I have said about him. And I know his mind. I know what the discovery of a treasure would mean to him. To you, it is only a means of earning a reward. To him…"

"Why do you…?"

"Please, let me finish. You do not understand why I feel as I do, after he made me into the cheat I was, to serve his purposes. But that is one of the reasons I am saying this. Can't you see how important it was to him, so important that he did what he did to me, whom he loved in his way—made me hate him, want to get away from him, made me dream only of freedom?" Ana Luz turned to face me, putting out her hand pleadingly. "You have already done so much. Can't you do this one other thing? Perhaps the manuscript *is* lost forever, and you are only wasting your time. If it is not, let him find it. Let him have the little glory of seeing his name on a printed card instead of yours. You already have seven hundred and fifty thousand *soles*. Does it make you a better man than he is because you are greedy for money while he is greedy for fame? Do you think…?"

"We met here," I said. "It's as good a place as any to say good-bye."

She shook her head.

"No. You are angry with me. I will not say good-bye to you this way."

"You can say good-bye any way you like. I don't want to hear anything else."

"Not that I am already more grateful to you than ever a woman was to a man before?" Her voice had changed, grown softer. "Not that if you did this one other thing that I ask, I would willingly spend my life paying you for it? Not that I would go anywhere you wished, do anything you wished, never ask for another thing…"

There was only one thing left for me to do. I reached into my pocket, took out the paper that had Martínez Castro's name on it, tore it in half, tore the halves across, and threw them away.

"Does that satisfy you?" I stood up. My throat was so tight that I thought I would choke. "If it does, stop talking of payments! I didn't buy a *criatura* from Naharro. I bought your freedom and gave it to you. You owe me nothing. You owe him nothing. You owe nobody anything, now, neither obedience nor gratitude nor loyalty. Naharro said it once, I say it again: You are your own mistress. You are free to do what you wish."

She looked up at me wordlessly. There was an expression on her face that I had never seen there before. It was almost—I don't know how to describe it. Shock isn't quite the word. It was more like a suspension of feeling than feeling itself, the kind of a blank look you see in a man's eyes during the few seconds after he has opened a telegram and the message is seeping in, when you can't tell whether he is going to laugh or cry or ask for a gun to blow his brains out or tell you that he has won the Irish Sweepstakes.

The anger grew on me. She had seen me throw away what might have been a fortune, and yet she still didn't realize that I was trying to cut her loose, once and for all, from any sense of obligation that remained in her mind. I said, "For God's sake, stop thinking like a *criatura!* Nobody owns you! Nobody is going to demand anything from you that you don't want to give! Can't you get it through your head that you are free—of Raul, of Naharro, of me, of everything! What more do you want?"

Her eyes closed for a moment. When they opened again, the dead look had left her face. She smiled.

"Nothing more."

She stood up, put her arms around my neck, pulled my head down, and kissed me.

The kiss lasted a long time. Somebody laughed, going by on the path. I didn't see who it was, because when Ana Luz finally let go of my neck and stepped back, no one was in sight. And I wasn't angry any more.

"That was not a payment." Her voice was low and quiet, almost sad. "You are a fine man, Al Colby. I will never forget you."

She turned away. I watched her slim figure, erect and graceful, disappear around a bend in the path before I sat down again. She didn't look back.

The breeze from the river picked up the pieces of paper I had torn and blew them across the grass. It still wasn't too late for me to go after them, but I let them go, thinking: The grapes were probably sour anyway.

Hope Julie can work things out for herself. Ana Luz will get along all right, as soon as she gets used to the feel of her wings. Fifty thousand dollars, a broken shoulder, and a kiss—no, two kisses. Good enough for a month's work. They were nice kisses, too. Wonder why Ana Luz sounded so sad…

The sun shining on the bench made me sleepy. I dozed off.